As she reached the bott
Marlowe scanned the

Tall. Broad. Dressed in a suit that hadn't been tailored but somehow fit him all the better for it. His dark head cocked at an arrogant angle, eyes the color of coffee traveled over her, scalp to feet.

A burst of society-bred outrage flooded her cheeks with heat.

The barest hint of a smile ghosted one corner of his mouth, though it failed to soften his expression.

She doubted anything could.

With his heavy-lidded bedroom eyes, the man looked distinctively...bad. The kind of bad that landed you in the back seats of cars. The kind of bad that kept you out past curfew. The kind of bad your mother warned you about.

Worse, she had the feeling that he not only knew this but was quietly enjoying it.

Without breaking eye contact, he lifted a cut crystal tumbler of amber liquid to his lips and took a leisurely sip.

And damned if she didn't feel that somehow it wasn't the drink he was tasting, but *her*.

* * *

Bad Boy with Benefits by Cynthia St. Aubin
is part of The Kane Heirs series.

Dear Reader,

When I say that I was excited to write book three in The Kane Heirs series, I mean that even while I was writing Marlowe's brother Mason's happily-ever-after in book two, I found myself having to politely send Marlowe and Law back to the waiting room when they kept whispering in my ear. Since it's finally their turn, I'm delighted to officially introduce them to you.

Marlowe Kane is a numbers girl, and something about Law Renaud just isn't adding up. Brawny and brooding, the owner of 4 Thieves distillery is less than thrilled when the beautiful billionaire heiress arrives to conduct an audit of their financial records for a Kane Foods acquisition.

When they're forced to share quarters due to an oncoming storm, sparks (and axes) fly. But their fling might come at a cost neither of them had expected. With the acquisition in jeopardy, Law stands to lose not only his livelihood but the dream he's chased since his troubled childhood. And if Marlowe isn't careful, the man who built 4 Thieves might just steal her heart.

Get comfy, grab your favorite beverage and enjoy!

Sweet reading!

Cynthia

CYNTHIA ST. AUBIN

—

BAD BOY WITH BENEFITS

HARLEQUIN
DESIRE

Recycling programs
for this product may
not exist in your area.

ISBN-13: 978-1-335-58149-5

Bad Boy with Benefits

Copyright © 2022 by Cynthia St. Aubin

For questions and comments about the quality of this book,
please contact us at CustomerService@Harlequin.com.

Harlequin Enterprises ULC
22 Adelaide St. West, 41st Floor
Toronto, Ontario M5H 4E3, Canada
www.Harlequin.com

Printed in U.S.A.

Cynthia St. Aubin wrote her first play at age eight and made her brothers perform it for the admission price of gum wrappers. When she was tall enough to reach the top drawer of her parents' dresser, she began pilfering her mother's secret stash of romance novels and has been in love with love ever since. A confirmed cheese addict, she lives in Texas with a handsome musician.

Books by Cynthia St. Aubin

The Kane Heirs

Corner Office Confessions
Secret Lives After Hours
Bad Boy with Benefits

Visit her Author Profile page at Harlequin.com, or cynthiastaubin.com, for more titles.

You can also find Cynthia St. Aubin on Facebook, along with other Harlequin Desire authors, at Facebook.com/harlequindesireauthors!

For Charles Griemsman,
editor extraordinaire and wonderful human.
Thank you.

Acknowledgments

First and foremost, my undying gratitude
to my husband, Ted, who puts up with the
semi-feral animal I become when I'm on deadline.
Thank you for leaving out a food bowl and
loving me even when I have mud on my paws.

Huge thanks go to Kerrigan Byrne,
my critique partner, emotional support human,
platonic life partner, adventure buddy
and fireside chatter. Me and thee.

My endless appreciation for my talented agent
lady and momma pit bull, Christine Witthohn,
who always believes.

Sincere gratitude to Melissa Carter,
who supplied ideas and inspiration
of the mathematical variety.
You are a scholar and a gentlewoman.

Finally, my heartfelt appreciation for readers
everywhere who make it possible for me
to do what I love. You are the glaze on my
doughnut and the cheese on my nachos.
You are the bestest.

One

Marlowe Kane stood on the second-floor landing of Fair Weather Hall, her face as hot as the marble balustrade was cool beneath her fingers. Early in her childhood, she'd learned this was the best place to spy on the lavish parties her parents frequently hosted. Then, she'd been small enough to peek through the gap between the curved miniature columns to the action below, hoping to see a stolen kiss. A graceful dance.

Now what she saw set her blood boiling.

Neil Campbell, her former fiancé, milling about the crowd accepting offered hors d'oeuvres and slim flutes of champagne in the grand hall before they made their way to the ballroom for the main event.

Another of her father's overblown current and prospective client schmooze-fests. An hours-long bacchanalia of caviar and canapés ending in scotch, cigars and much masculine backslapping.

Still, to her great irritation, predominantly a boys' club.

Why Neil was attending after what he'd done, Marlowe couldn't comprehend.

She wished Samuel and Mason were here.

Only a year older, her twin brothers had always been her self-appointed protectors, though their methodologies differed wildly.

Samuel, who could reduce anyone to a quaking, apologetic heap with a calculated verbal disemboweling, and Mason, who tended to swing first and settle out of court later.

But with Samuel firmly anchored in the plans for his impending nuptials to his high school crush and Mason completely consumed by his new relationship with their father's executive assistant, both had proved elusive.

Which was a shame, as their vibrant dislike for her former fiancé had been one of the few topics on which they wholeheartedly agreed.

Releasing her death grip on the balustrade, Marlowe took a deep, bracing breath and began to descend the stairs.

With each step, she walked astride younger versions of herself who had done the same with varying degrees of enthusiasm.

Christmas mornings. High school dates. Polo matches. Her mother's funeral. The New Year's Eve party where she'd met Neil Campbell two years ago.

Neil had been handsome in his tuxedo, his dark hair glazed with a bluish sheen in the moonlight. The pinkish glow on his high cheekbones and the tip of his straight, patrician nose hinted that he'd been out there for a while.

Before the evening was over, they were bonding over shared tales of their domineering fathers—old friends, as it turned out.

That first meeting turned into a first date, and then a quick courtship heartily encouraged by both their fathers, and soon they were engaged. He'd been so different in those early days. Spontaneous. Romantic. Adventurous. Dashing, even.

Something had changed—and quickly—when her father, president and chairman emeritus of the Philadelphia-based, billion-dollar Kane Foods International empire, had taken Neil under his iron wing. Marlowe hadn't begrudged him this. After all, she'd spent the majority of her life chasing what her fiancé had been freely given.

Her father's approval.

It had become Neil's drug of choice.

His days at the office grew longer, his temper shorter, his kisses more perfunctory. She'd stopped dreaming about wedding plans and wondered where the passion had gone.

Discovering he'd been following her father's executive assistant around and sending her creepy texts had been the proverbial straw that broke the camel's back. A disturbing turn of events that her father had been present for. It was only four weeks ago that everything had fallen apart.

Which brought her back to her original question.

What the hell was Neil doing here?

As she reached the bottom step of the grand staircase, Marlowe scanned the crowd, searching for the unmistakable pewter-colored crown of her father's hair.

Instead, she spotted not her father nor Neil, but *him*.

Tall. Broad. Dressed in a suit that hadn't been tailored but somehow fit him all the better for it. His dark head cocked at an arrogant angle, eyes the color of coffee traveled over her, scalp to foot.

A burst of society-bred outrage flooded her cheeks with heat. Men liked looking at her. Long years enduring the furtive, grabby glances at endless corporate mixers and cocktail parties had acquainted her with this irrefutable fact.

But a man who didn't even *try* to observe the social pantomime of pretending not to?

Never.

The barest hint of a shadow ghosted one corner of his mouth, though it failed to soften his expression one iota.

Though she doubted anything could.

His face actively scorned the complimentary adjectives most common to the men of her acquaintance.

Good-looking? Hardly.

With his heavy-lidded bedroom eyes, the man looked distinctively…bad. The kind of bad that landed you in the back seats of cars. The kind of bad that kept you out past curfew. The kind of bad your mother warned you about.

Handsome? Decidedly not.

With the jaw like broken granite, sharp cheekbones and an aquiline nose one fight too many had nudged slightly left of plumb, his features spit at symmetry.

Attractive?

The scowl perma-welded to his face seemed designed to do precisely the opposite. His expression, the equivalent of a No Trespassing sign.

Taken together, it was a visual collision, and she found herself struggling to tear her eyes away.

Worse, she had the feeling that he not only knew this but was quietly enjoying it.

Without breaking eye contact, he lifted a crystal tumbler of amber liquid to his lips and took a leisurely sip.

And damned if she didn't feel that, somehow, it wasn't the drink he was tasting, but *her*.

With as much hauteur as she could summon, Marlowe lifted her chin and turned her gaze deliberately away before stepping off the last stair and slipping into the crowd.

She gratefully accepted a glass of champagne from the first silver-tray-bearing server she encountered, relishing the cold, acidic bite.

"I've been looking for you," a voice said just behind her.

Marlowe's body stiffened out of reflex. She wasn't entirely sure when this had become her default reaction to her former fiancé but knew it predated the business with Charlotte by several months.

"Hello, Neil." Fingers wrapped tightly around her champagne flute, she turned to face him.

He had always looked his best in a suit and tonight was no different. This evening's ensemble was deep blue, beautifully cut and undoubtedly expensive. But something about the juxtaposition of her once-fiancé and the arrogant, unpretentious masculinity of the man across the room made Neil look…fussy by comparison. His hair was a little too neatly styled, his eyebrows slightly overgroomed, his crisp white shirt too pristine.

"Surprised to see me?" Lines of amusement crinkled the corners of his eyes as he lifted a martini to his lips and suppressed a slight grimace.

Marlowe had long suspected Neil didn't like them so much as he liked how he looked holding them.

"I'm not sure *surprised* is the word I would have chosen," she said, taking another sip of her champagne.

"Well, you haven't been answering my calls, so I had to resort to more creative measures." His easy smile revealed a row of perfectly straight white teeth.

"So you decided to crash a client event?" Marlowe began to walk, knowing he would fall into step beside her.

"Who's crashing? I came as my father's guest."

Henry Campbell, London-born, painfully posh and senior partner of Campbell Capital, had proved a significant stumbling block when it came to disentangling herself from her engagement. While Parker Kane's approbation could be fickle where Campbell's son was concerned, his devotion to the investment banker and the significant funds he controlled remained ever ardent and unfailingly faithful.

"Then maybe you should keep him company," she suggested, cutting her eyes toward the bar, where Henry Campbell could reliably be found.

Neil took a quick step and turned to block her path. "I need to talk to you."

"No," Marlowe said, slipping past him. "You don't."

"Marlowe, *please*."

It was the *please* that caught her. Urgent and spoken with more sincere emotion than she'd heard from him in at least a year.

"Five minutes of your time," he said, eyes earnest and empty of his usual expectant surety. "That's all I'm asking."

She hesitated, glancing toward the wall where she'd

spotted the mystery man, oddly disappointed when she found it empty. "All right."

Neil led them away from the main hall and down a side corridor to a balcony off the family's private dining room. Not the precise place where they'd first met, but an obvious and somewhat cringey attempt at re-creating the mood.

He swung open a French door and waited for her to walk through before shutting it behind them.

Marlowe moved to the waist-high brick wall and leaned her forearms against the gritty surface, her drink still clutched in her hand as she looked out on the gardens below. Built by her great-grandfather in the late 1800s, Fair Weather Hall had acres of sprawling green lawn encircled by a thick border of trees that kept it stubbornly secluded from the world beyond.

"Isn't it beautiful?" Neil stood several paces away, gazing at the stars overhead as if to encourage her to do the same.

"Why did you want to talk to me?" she asked, a pin aimed at the balloon of his hopeful, romantic interlude.

"Us, of course."

A heavy sigh deflated her chest. "Neil, there is no *us*."

He took several steps closer, his eyes darting to her hand. "If that's true, why are you still wearing the ring?"

Shit.

Marlowe had been so shocked to see him, she'd completely forgotten she was wearing it. She'd kept it on when attending social gatherings to fend off unwanted advances from would-be suitors.

"Here," she said, setting aside her champagne glass

to wiggle it off her finger and hold it out to him on an open palm. "You can have it back."

Neil brushed Marlowe's hair from her cheekbone. "It's not the ring I want back. It's *you*."

Jerking away, she shook her head in disgust. "How can you even think I would consider getting back with you after what you did?"

"You're going to throw everything we had away just because I sent your father's assistant a few anonymous texts warning her about Mason?" He chuckled as if what he'd said represented the most negligible of complaints.

"One of which you sent while parked near her home over an hour outside the city," she reminded him.

Neil drained his martini and set the glass on a stone planter. "I'm not saying what I did was right. I'm saying I was only trying to look out for someone in a vulnerable position."

Marlowe suppressed an eye roll. "It may shock you to know that I'm amply familiar with the tactics of gaslighting and mansplaining, so if your plan for convincing me to take you back involves either, I would strongly urge you to reconsider."

Arms folded across his chest, Neil leaned against the railing next to her. "Weren't *you* the one who came to *me* because you were worried about Mason?"

This part had been true.

She and Mason had always been closer than she and Samuel, and Mason's sudden retreat from her had set her sisterly antennae twitching. When he started showing up to work with the occasional subtly concealed bruise, she'd begun to worry. When she'd noticed large withdrawals from his personal checking account, she had begun to worry *a lot*.

"Sharing my concerns about my brother isn't tanta-mount to giving you permission to access private, fam-ily financial information or to warn Charlotte about becoming involved with him."

"I know that." He placed his hand over her wrist, a part of her he had always claimed to admire. "What I did was invasive and stupid. I just got too…involved."

She stretched out her fingers, once again offering him the ring. "So did I."

Desperation dug a crease between his dark eyebrows. "Marlowe, this is our dream. A family dynasty. The Kanes and the Campbells, just like we always talked about."

"Just like *you* always talked about." And for a while, she had listened. Buying into his lush narrative of the life they would build together. Their dream wedding. Travel. And eventually, children.

As soon as he ascended to his rightful place within Kane Foods with the help of his father's investment.

Only, the wedding date seemed to retreat further and further into the distance, taking her hopes along with it. Now, with her brother's nuptials careening toward her like a freight train, Marlowe realized how gullible she had been to wait all this time.

"Take it," she urged.

Neil looked at the diamond-studded ring twinkling like a miniature star in her outstretched palm. The hope-ful light in his eyes blinked out, leaving something flat and cold in its place. "How about a goodbye kiss, then? For closure."

The first filament of fear sizzled in Marlowe's stom-ach as she realized just how alone they were on this side of the house. With the din filling the great hall, she could scream at the top of her lungs and not a soul would hear her.

"No, Neil." She took a step backward.

"Remember you used to tell me how much this turned you on?" His hand flashed out and buried itself in the hair at her nape, tightening until she felt her scalp prickle.

Marlowe shoved her hands against his chest as hard as she could. "Neil, I said—"

The kiss was as brief as it was brutal. His mouth crushed against hers hard enough that she felt the shape of his teeth against her lips, then was gone abruptly as a low, pained grunt doubled Neil in half.

Marlowe's heart pounded in her ears as she pressed her fingers to her lips, half expecting to find them smeared with blood. When they showed clean, she looked beyond them and saw what had happened.

Him.

The man who had stared at her.

Here, on the balcony. He had a hold of Neil by the front of his shirt, his massive fist gripping the no-longer-pristine fabric as he towered over him.

"She said *no*." His words were not spoken but hewed. Pried from a throat rusty with disuse. "You understand consent?" he growled, hauling her former fiancé upward, only the tips of his mirror-polished loafers making contact with the balcony tiles.

Neil glared at him through eyes made reptilian by spite. "Yes."

"Good." He eased his hold slightly. "Now, are you going to leave, or do I need to throw your preppy ass off this balcony?"

"I'll leave," he croaked.

The man opened his fist, and Neil staggered several steps before recovering his self-assured posture. He took the time to smooth his shirt and cast a long, meaningful look in Marlowe's direction before exiting through the French doors.

When he was gone, the man turned to her, eyes moving over her body just as brazenly but with clinical concern. "You okay?"

Marlowe ran a shaking hand over her rumpled hair, a fizzy cocktail of adrenaline, irritation and fear coursing through her body. "I'm fine."

He took a step closer, looking like he might be on the point of conducting a physical examination. "Are you sure?"

"Yes," she snapped. "You can go now."

His jaw hardened as he raised an eyebrow at her. "Is that right?"

A balmy breeze swept through the colonnade, bringing with it the scent of roses and rain. Ludicrously ill-suited to the moment.

"Yes." She turned from him to retrieve her champagne. "Despite the fact that you clearly don't belong to my father's crowd, I'm assuming you have *some* reason for attending this event aside from lurking on balconies and ogling me."

As soon as the words were out of her mouth, Marlowe wanted to recall them. Humiliation always sharpened her tongue in ways she didn't like but could never seem to prevent.

His hulking form shadowed her peripheral vision. "You forgot saving you from your prick of a fiancé."

"*Saving* me?" The word triggered a stinging snap of anger deep within her solar plexus. "You basically strip me naked with your eyes, you follow us out here from the hall like some kind of creeper, then you ride in like Rambo without my having asked for your interference or your help. Tell me, am I supposed to swoon or throw you a parade? I'm fairly experienced when it comes to bolstering the egos of billionaires, but I'm a little unclear about cocktail reception *vigilantes*."

His dress shirt stretched taut over his mounded biceps as he crossed his arms over his chest, a posture that somehow looked more defensive than defiant. "First, if you don't think I noticed the way you were looking at me, you're either blind or high. Second, you're saying you would have preferred that I leave you alone with *Neil*?"

He spit the name like it was battery acid on his tongue.

"I'm saying I'm tired of men putting me in situations so that other men can congratulate themselves for rescuing me," she said, deliberately ignoring the first part of his statement.

Because it had been true.

It still was.

Even as she stoked the engines of her righteous indignation, she fought to keep her eyes from drinking in additional details offered up by his proximity. The thin, silvery scar interrupted the peak of his left eyebrow. The subtle trench in the skin of his cheekbone. The ludicrous length of his dark lashes. The way proximity to his huge, hulking form touched a primal part of her brain devoted to feelings of safety.

Warmth radiated through the fabric of his dress shirt, kissing her bare arm. "I know that isolating a woman from the safety of a crowd is a classic tactic of a predator. I know that shifting blame for shitty behavior is the hallmark of a narcissist. I know that any man who would put his hands on a woman deserves to have his spleen ripped out. And I know that no amount of beauty can make up for being a conceited, dismissive elitist with a silver spoon stuck where the sun doesn't shine."

Marlowe blinked at him, her mouth open in shock. A flood of lame rejoinders invaded her mind, each more cliché than the last and all of the how-dare-you variety.

Before she could make any of them exit her lips, he bent and picked up the engagement ring she hadn't even realized she'd dropped.

Taking her hand in his, he turned it palm up and placed the ring squarely in the center. Large, warm and deliciously rough, his fingers closed over hers, the diamond's intricate setting gently biting into her fist. He held it a beat longer than necessary, his gaze smoldering into hers.

Tingling awareness traveled up her arm and systematically woke every nerve center in her body until it felt like her heart beat not just in her chest but in her lips, skin and navel.

When he let go, the sudden loss of warmth and compression left her feeling strangely abandoned and cold despite the late-summer heat.

"Enjoy the rest of your evening."

The rough, low words lingered like smoke long after he'd turned on his heel and left her pulsing in his wake.

Marlowe wasn't sure which surprised her more.

That she'd allowed him to have the last word, or that she wanted more of them.

More of him.

Two

Marlowe Kane.

Laurent "Law" Renaud sat at the desk in the hayloft that had been become the de facto office when he and his brother converted the old barn into the first building of 4 Thieves distillery. On the screen of the laptop before him were the results of a Google search that had prompted him to hop from All to Images almost immediately.

Marlowe in a power suit, posing with her father and brothers at Kane Foods headquarters. Marlowe in a black couture gown at a black-tie benefit for cancer research. Marlowe sunning herself on the deck of a yacht, facedown and with the straps of her bikini top undone.

This last had clearly been captured from a distance that suggested the long-angle lens of a paparazzo. She had been linked to a billionaire European media mogul at the time, Law read with an acid surge of displeasure.

He had lingered on that photo the longest, mentally running a hand along the elegant dip at the center of her spine, up the graceful curve of her neck and out over shoulders he knew would be tight, even when she was supposed to be relaxing.

Startled by a high, shrill wolf whistle, Law slapped the laptop closed. He glanced over his shoulder to see his brother Remy grinning like the Cheshire cat on the landing at the top of the stairs, a stack of shipping orders in one hand.

"And who was that you're pretending not to have been cyberstalking?" he asked, setting the papers on the corner of Law's desk.

Third in the lineup of Charles "Zap" Renaud's four sons, Remy had inherited their father's coal-black hair and piercing gray eyes. Though he stood a few inches shorter than Law, manual labor had packed muscle onto his six-foot-two frame. A fact he liked to advertise by living life almost exclusively in well-worn jeans and T-shirts.

"No one important," Law grumbled.

"Then you won't mind sharing." Remy leaned over and flipped the laptop open, his dark eyebrows lifting appreciatively when Marlowe's face appeared.

Desire punched Law low and deep in the groin, just as it had the first time he'd seen her descending the stairs at Fair Weather Hall.

Her insolent cheekbones. The high, fine tilt of her head. Her eyes the pale blue of polar ice. Her hair a shimmering, sharp-edged platinum curtain echoing her jawline. A body assembled in elegant planes and angles, moving beneath the thin, silvery fabric of her dress.

She had looked like a Valkyrie. A warrior goddess.

Law had stood there, dumb as a stump, the bumbling, backwoods boy who had seen his first Ferrari, unable to tear his eyes away. The defiant way she'd challenged his gaze with one just as intense and unapologetic only inflamed him further.

"Not your usual type," Remy assessed, squinting at the screen. "But she has that whole ice-princess-begging-to-be— Holy shit." His brother jerked upright abruptly. "She's a *Kane*?"

"Yeah," Law said.

"Holy shit," Remy repeated. Leaning in again, he used the mouse to rapidly scroll through the images Law had spent the better part of his morning perusing instead of the work he was meant to be doing. "She single?"

Law slapped his brother's hand away. "None of your goddamn business."

Truly, he didn't know the answer to that himself, despite what he had witnessed the night before. A flash of rage shot through him at the memory. He had watched them first as they had met in the crowd, the obvious displeasure on Marlowe's face, the guarded posture and body language. When he saw how she had been herded away, Law had followed and, finding another set of doors at the opposite end of the balcony, observed from a safe distance.

It had taken every ounce of restraint he owned not to tear off the arm her fiancé had grabbed her with.

"How did it go last night?" Remy slouched into the chair at the desk overlooking the rows of gleaming copper-pot stills beyond the railing his brother had built using wood salvaged from an old church on the property. Purchased while he and Remy had both still been working months at a time on an offshore oil rig and funneling every available penny into their dream, the twenty-acre parcel of land had been their first major investment in the distillery's construction. And they had used every scrap of wood and metal on the property, as was the Renaud way.

Waste not, his father had always said, always leaving off the second half of the adage. Whether because *want not* was implied or because Zap Renaud knew it had never applied to him or his four sons, Law didn't know.

Because they *had* wanted.

For the mother who had walked out when Law was twelve. For money. For a lot of things. Though food had never been one of them, even if their father had his sons resort to…*creative* methods of acquiring it on occasion.

That creativity hadn't been solely dedicated to food and had come to affect his and his brothers' lives in a variety of negative ways. Incarceration one of them.

The youngest of the four, Law held the distinction of being the only Renaud who had never served time. With his father ten years dead, and the distillery finally in the black, it had appeared the Renaud luck was finally changing.

Until recently.

Law shrugged, stretching his long legs as he turned his attention to his brother. "He wants to send someone out here to audit our financial records."

The conversation had been as brief as it was predictable. Seething from the physical confrontation and too much time spent in the presence of the money-luxe assholes whose faces made his fist itch, Law had run into Parker Kane while making a beeline for the exit.

Pretending to lament Law's early departure, Kane had casually mentioned that *prospective partnerships like theirs* typically *bore additional discovery.*

A comment specifically designed to remind Law how fortunate 4 Thieves was to even be *considered* for a Kane partnership.

Remy's jaw tightened. "I thought we already sent them everything they needed, electronically."

"We did," Law said.

"Then why the hell would he need to send someone out here?"

Pushing himself up from his chair, Law paced over to the railing, simultaneously taking comfort in the feeling of the solid, silky wood and the sight of the bustling hive of activity below.

"He doesn't. He just wants us to know that he can shine a flashlight up our collective hindquarters anytime he feels like it."

Remy was silent for a protracted moment. "You don't think he could be reconsidering, do you?"

The concern in his brother's voice gnawed at Law's gut.

They'd worked so hard to build 4 Thieves. Poured their blood, sweat and every available resource into the business. To pull the four Renaud brothers out of generations of suffering and build a lasting legacy. He had chosen the name for that specific reason. To acknowledge their checkered past and turn it into a legitimate future.

The irony that one of his brothers would have nothing to do with what remained of the family and another had jeopardized their plans for expansion still burned like an acid bath. And now they were in the precarious position of needing funding to continue.

Enter Parker Kane, who had miraculously approached them about expanding their distribution at precisely the right time.

Remy had balked at the much-larger offer, wanting to go with one of the more modest options. But once Law had begun to think about what he could do with that kind of money, he couldn't let it go.

"I know he wants 4 Thieves under the Kane Foods umbrella. I just don't know *why*." That had been the chief source of Law's hesitation, despite how badly he wanted the growth an infusion of cash would bring. Also, the reason he had decided to attend last night's billionaire circle-jerk in the first place.

He had needed to look Parker Kane in the eye. To *take the measure of the man*, as his father had called it. But he'd left feeling he'd been the one who'd been found lacking.

Which pissed him off to no end.

As if the money you earned with the sweat of your own brow spent any differently than dollars passed down from Daddy.

"Did you agree to the audit?" Remy asked, flicking the stubble on his neck and jaw with the backs of his fingernails.

"I did," Law said. "That's why I was doing some digging on Marlowe Kane. *She's* the one doing the honors."

Not exactly a bold-faced lie, but not the naked truth either. Were anyone to do a forensic analysis on the search-engine time stamp, they'd find Marlowe's name in the results a good hour before he'd gotten the email from Parker Kane's assistant.

"She's coming *here*?" Excitement glazed Remy's eyes with a *kid-on-Christmas-morning* glow.

Not that Christmases in the Renaud house had ever generated that particular brand of enthusiasm.

"Next Monday. And under no circumstances will you so much as twitch a testicle in her direction. Understand?" Law pointed a finger at his brother's already-smirking face.

Remy's reputation as a ladies' man had been established early and well in Terrebonne Parish, where they'd grown up, and had followed them to Fincastle, Virginia. These days, the encounters tended to be brief and exclusively contained to women who caught his eye while passing through the distillery. Why the thought of Marlowe being one of these should produce a stab of irrational jealousy, Law didn't know.

After all, it hadn't been *Remy* who had charmed the panties off Law's ex-girlfriend.

Quickly sweeping the thought away, Law crossed to the coffee maker and refilled the riotously painted—if somewhat oddly shaped—mug his niece had proudly presented to him on his birthday.

"I solemnly swear to keep my eyes, hands and all other appendages to myself," Remy said, palm raised as if he were on the witness stand.

"Good." Lifting the mug to his lips, Law sipped, grimacing at the bitter brew.

"Emily?" Remy asked with a knowing smile.

Though he appreciated his eight-year-old niece's dedication to rising early and sneaking into the office to make coffee, neither he nor Remy had the heart to tell her it wasn't meant to be chewed. Latent guilt, Law suspected, on the part of two grown men who had raised her after Emily's mother—Remy's ex-wife—took off shortly after her birth.

Another example in the long line of terrible Renaud luck where romantic partners were concerned.

"Isn't there any way you can get here first in the mornings?" Law asked.

"I've tried." Remy shrugged. "She resets my alarm."

"Don't you lock your phone?"

"Of course I do," his brother said. "She always manages to figure out the passcode."

"I swear that kid is some kind of savant." Law choked down another gritty sip, pausing on the way to his desk as the first tendrils of an idea began unfurling. "Speaking of, do you think you can have someone look after her for a couple hours this weekend?"

"Emily?" Remy asked. "Why?"

Setting the unwieldy mug on his desk, Law returned his attention to the image of Marlowe's elegant, austerely beautiful face.

As the youngest, Law had often been assigned the role of sentinel on their covert operations. Alerting his brothers when the beam of a flashlight or the glow of headlights swung their way. The one time he'd failed, Remy had lost five years to a correctional facility.

Law had been on the lookout for trouble ever since.

Or thought he had.

Because of his insistence on pursuing Kane Foods' investment to the exclusion of all others, he'd invited trouble directly to their door.

While he couldn't stop Marlowe Kane from coming, he could make it so she didn't want to stay any longer than necessary.

Given how she'd hitchhiked a ride in his head all

the way back from Philadelphia, it was probably best for them both.

Tearing his eyes away from the screen, he smiled at Remy. "I have some special preparations in mind."

Three

You've got to be kidding me.

The words appeared first in Marlowe's mind, then found their way to her mouth—which had been hanging open in shock prior to her speaking them.

Shock, at the sight greeting her beyond the blue-tinted windshield of her dust-coated BMW.

A man.

A *shirtless* man.

A shirtless man *swinging an axe*.

None of these facts taken alone would represent a problem.

If the shirtless, axe-swinging man wasn't Laurent Renaud, owner of 4 Thieves distillery.

Laurent Renaud, owner of 4 Thieves distillery *and* the impromptu balcony-Batman who had manhandled Neil before denting her ego with a verbal two-by-four.

Not that she hadn't deserved it.

Having come to this realization after an additional glass of head-cooling champagne, she'd made her way to the ballroom, hoping to find him and apologize. He had been trying to help, after all. Even if his display of brute strength had been vulgar, unnecessary...and perhaps the teeniest bit erotic.

When he was nowhere to be found, she'd left the party early and returned home to her Rittenhouse Square townhome, where a long bath and trash TV had been her solace.

The following morning, her father had called her into his office to inform her she would be conducting an on-site audit of the 4 Thieves distillery's financial records, suggesting that surely she should be able to uncover *something* that supported a valuation *better reflecting their level of commitment.*

Parker Kane's equivalent of King's Gambit in the long chess match of their negotiations.

Despite her initial reservations, the idea of escaping the marble-choked confines of the Kane Foods corporate headquarters in downtown Philadelphia appealed to her. After the long, strange month she'd spent burying herself in work following her broken engagement and the subsequent dustup with Neil, it sounded downright therapeutic.

Right up until she'd rumbled over the dirt road ribboning through towering stands of oak and maple trees to find a half-naked man cleaving large chunks of wood outside the distillery's smokehouse.

She watched in rapt fascination as Renaud bent to grab another tawny block, the muscles of his broad, bare back working in a symphony as he placed it on the stump. Long arms swinging overhead, large hands gripping the thick handle and bringing it down with a percussive *whack* and a guttural grunt that left her feeling just as cleaved.

"You've *got* to be kidding me," she repeated.

Chills danced over her arms as she watched the brutal grace of his arc against the lilting swell of classical music emanating from the speakers of her state-of-the-art sound system. As had often been the case when confronting an especially unpleasant task, she had played it exclusively during her five-hour journey from Philly. Rejecting her father's offer of a private jet owned by Kane Foods International, she had opted for a mini, solo road trip, thinking the car time would give her a chance to clear her head and calm her nerves.

Which had actually worked until—

Whack.

The pelvic floor her yoga instructor was always nagging her to tighten seized in a furious, involuntary clench. Apparently, the secret to the perfect handstand wasn't core control, but a sweaty woodsman.

A sweaty woodsman who had turned and was now staring directly at her.

Shit.

Any desperate thoughts she'd had about peeling out in a spray of gravel and heading straight home evaporated abruptly.

She turned off the engine and, feeling the burn of his gaze on her, abandoned a last self-check in the rearview mirror—she'd be damned if she'd let him be privy to this small but very characteristic vanity. Reaching into the passenger seat, she gathered the leather satchel containing her laptop and draped her trench coat over her arm before exiting the car and hip checking the door closed behind her.

On poorly chosen designer heels, she picked her way over to him, spine ramrod straight, shoulders rolled back and chin tipped at the imperious angle she'd mastered at her father's elbow.

She stopped a polite distance away, half-afraid she might end up toppling forward from the sheer gravitational magnetism.

"Hello again," she said.

Gravel crunched under his work boots as he shifted his weight, one massive arm flexing to rest the blunt side of the axe in the dip where his sinewy neck fed into the sloping mound of his shoulder.

"So, you're Laurent Renaud, I take it?"

He sucked his teeth and held out the non-axe-bearing hand. "Law."

Her palm disappeared into his grip, producing a familiar jolt the second his roughened skin touched hers. So unlike the endless parade of deferentially limp handshakes from men used to gripping golf clubs and the handles of designer briefcases. Always folding around her hand like it was a bird they were afraid to crush.

"Look," she said, plunging headlong into the inevitable awkwardness. "About the night we met—"

"We didn't." He released her hand and let his swing loose by his side, obviously more at ease on his home territory. "At least, I don't remember you telling me your name. Or asking for mine."

"You're right," she allowed. "And that was rude of me. I was very upset, but I regret speaking to you the way that I did."

"Which part?" Dark brows gathered toward each

other beneath a tumble of equally dark hair stuck to his sun-beaten but smooth forehead by a sheen of sweat. Within the parenthetical stubble of a lazily shaped goatee, his disproportionately full lips turned downward.

She couldn't decide if he genuinely didn't remember or he just wanted to make her say it again and wasn't sure which was worse.

"About you staring at me and following me like a creeper and being a—" she hesitated, swallowing around a dry throat before continuing "—cocktail reception vigilante."

"I believe you said *stripping you naked with my eyes*," he corrected. "And you were right." He let the admission hang there, thickening the air between them. "What's your point?"

Biting down on a flicker of irritation, Marlowe reached deep for the diplomacy she'd perfected in so many antagonistic executive discussions. "My point is, I think maybe we *both* said some things—out of anger—that we might not have, given different circumstances."

"Is this an apology?" he asked. "Because you could have just started with that and saved us some time."

She wanted to scream.

A single bead of sweat spilled over the indentation at the base of his neck, crawling down his sternum to the dangerous ridge between his abdominals, disappearing into the waistband of Carhartt work pants the color of dried tobacco leaves.

He had watched her watch it.

The final straw tossed on the heap of irritation his taciturn attitude and frank assessment of her had piled up.

"You know what? Never mind. If you'll just show me to your office, we can get this over with."

Law's lips twitched, his knuckles whitening as his grip tightened. Without warning, he buried the blade in the stump next to her with a swift stroke that made her jump.

"Follow me."

He stalked away from her around the corner of the wood-paneled building, rust spreading like lichen in uneven patches on the corrugated tin roof. From a chimney near its pitched peak, a bluish column ribboned up against the deep, exhausted green of late-summer leaves, the rich scent of smoked meat heavy on the air.

Crunching along behind him, Marlowe used the opportunity to covertly examine the wide wings of muscle beneath his shoulder blades, appreciating the way they narrowed at his waist. Just as she appreciated the way his not-too-loose/not-too-light work pants hinted at the rounded gluteal muscles beneath. Awash in a sea of bespoke suits from the time she could walk, she couldn't remember a single pair of trousers that worshipped their wearer this efficiently.

They walked in silence broken only by the sound of their syncopated footfalls and the rush of wind through the surrounding trees. The rare kind of quiet she hadn't experienced since she'd sneaked away during a family ski trip to Aspen when she was twelve.

Past the smokehouse, Marlowe found herself mesmerized by the sprawl of lush green, rising into a gentle hill, at the top of which sat an old farmhouse, somehow stately in its weathered beauty. A large, blocky metal-sided warehouse sat tucked back farther on the property. The distillery, she guessed, given the winding gravel road snaking its way to a flat patch where several cars and trucks were parked.

Between this and where she stood were scattered

lavender gardens, fenced vegetable patches, a corral where several horses lazily chewed at the long, silky grass growing around the fence posts.

So unlike the meticulously manicured grounds of Fair Weather Hall.

Disorganized. Unplanned. Wild.

"Coming?"

Law had stopped on the path before her, his swiveled torso revealing the ladder of his ribs below the thick wall of his chest.

Tightening her grip on her satchel, Marlowe refused to hurry to catch up, a flare of alarm rising in her when she realized where he was headed.

She had seen ATVs before. Had actually ridden in one while at the family's Willow Creek Winery in Napa. *This* was not an ATV. The vehicle—a term she applied *very* loosely—parked behind the smokehouse was some unholy union of a golf cart and dune buggy. Assembled with an odd conglomeration of parts that had obviously belonged to other machines in their previous lives, it looked somehow…embarrassed of the brand-new, disproportionately large knobby tires affixed to its frame.

Law slid into the driver's seat with an ease surprising for his size. Black smoke belched out near the rear of the undercarriage as he turned over the engine.

Noting that she had failed to join him, Law lifted an eyebrow at her.

"Where are we going?" she shouted over the motor's erratic rumble, still rooted to the spot.

He jerked his chin toward the large metal warehouse. "There."

She took a step backward. "I can just drive my car—"

"No," he barked. "You can't."

A hot-blue pilot flame of anger ignited in her head. Even with the considerable privilege of her upbringing, an MBA from Yale and a hard-fought battle to executive management, it was amazing how often men still assumed she could be *told*.

"Look, I understand that you don't really want me here, and believe it or not, I'm not exactly overjoyed myself. But you can at least offer me basic civility if not common courtesy. Wanting to drive my own vehicle to the place where I'll be working is an exceedingly reasonable request, and I expect it to be honored."

Her throat felt hot from the effort of raising her voice to be heard, her chest tight with a potent mix of adrenaline and righteous fury.

Law's jaw flexed as he chewed the inside of his cheek. "See that dip in the road?"

She followed his gaze to where the winding gravel disappeared below the rise, only to appear again at the base of the hill beyond.

"Yes," she said.

"My brother lost half a load of scrap metal just below it on the way to the dump. Unless that coupe of yours has titanium tires, I'd recommend you get in."

The barest hint of an accent haunted his words, loosening the surprisingly articulate cadence of his delivery.

"If that's true," she said, looking toward the small parking lot, "how did *they* get up there?"

"*They*," he said, mimicking her pointed pronunciation, "live here."

Had there been another truck bearing a dump-bound load of scrap metal tearing down the hill at that precise second, Marlowe might have been tempted to throw herself in front of it.

"I see." She sniffed, rewarded by a sinus-full of oily exhaust as she took the seat beside his, knees glued primly together as his big body occupied approximately 75 percent of the available real estate. On a warm breeze, she caught a current of his scent. Clean sweat, cedar, the ghost of resiny soap or shampoo. Combined with his nearness, it made her feel dizzy. Strangely buzzed.

She cleared her throat in hopes it might clear her head as well. "Ready when you—"

The buggy leaped forward, and Marlowe yelped, her hands flying out to steady herself, one of them landing on Law's steely thigh, mere inches from his crotch. She flinched as she would from a hot stove, noting the flicker of a smile creasing the corner of his lips.

"Sorry about that," he said. "She's a little fussy in first."

Finally locating a handle on the metal frame, she white-knuckle clutched it. "I'm sure."

Law's large hand gripped the rounded knob of a gearshift, the ropes of muscle in his forearms flexing as he wrestled it backward and out, knuckles nearly grazing the bare skin of her leg.

"Who the hell built this thing anyway?" she asked.

"My brother Remy." As if on cue, he lifted a hand, looking past her. She turned to see a dark-haired man in jeans and a white undershirt lifting debris from a pile into the bed of a large black truck. Sturdily built though lacking several inches of Law's height, the resemblance was clear.

They swung wide to avoid an old tractor tire, and the force sent her torso lurching sideways where her arm brushed against his, coming away kissed by his sweat.

Awareness of the contact crackled on her skin where the breeze cooled it.

The twitch of revulsion she'd always felt when Neil, damp in his tennis whites, insisted on pawing her after a match failed to materialize.

Interesting.

"And is 'Remy' short for something as well?"

"'Pain in the ass,'" Law grunted. "Or 'Rainier.'"

Marlowe quickly banished a small smile from her face. Of pain-in-the-ass brothers, she knew *nothing.* Especially not the variety that fell madly, wildly in love and seemed to forget her existence entirely. They'd made the perfunctory calls in the wake of her breakup with Neil, the appropriately soothing noises when they were all together. But in her experience, new love instinctively recoiled from heartbreak. As if romantic discord were contagious.

A fact that her brother Samuel's wedding to his fiancée, Arlie Banks, a mere month hence, had brought painfully to the fore.

Another bump nearly rocketed her from her seat, her rear end briefly floating before coming down with enough force to send a jolt of pain singing along her spine.

She winced with the intensity of it, surprised when the buggy slowed.

"You okay?" he asked.

"Fine," she said, nodding quickly. "Old injury."

"Cheerleading?" He stepped on the gas again, but at an incrementally reduced pace.

Marlowe rolled her eyes. True, but not her primary athletic pursuit.

"I've always been curious," she said, leaning in to

make sure none of her words were lost. "Who determines which joke the entire male species is going to recycle at any given time? Is there some sort of newsletter, or…?"

Minute crinkles etched the corner of his eye. "Rugby?"

"Polo, actually."

He made a noise that conveyed both surprise and begrudging respect.

She'd heard it often.

The assumptions were painfully predictable and rarely varied. Volleyball. Gymnastics. Ballet. Any of the other sports that men somehow managed to devalue and sexualize at the same time.

Polo had been her father's influence, of course. As cerebral Samuel had no interest in sports and Mason's chief athletic pursuit was chasing women, it had fallen to her to carry on the Kane legacy. Like her father and his father before him.

Carry it she had.

Until the long line of blue ribbons halted abruptly in her seventeenth year with the terrible accident that had ended both her and her horse's career.

Law geared the buggy down as they bypassed what looked to be the main entrance, on the side of the building where the cars were parked, and rattled over yet another gravel path to the south end. A set of rickety steps led to a badly used door pocked with what she hoped were *not* bullet holes and smudged by boot prints at the bottom where it had been kicked closed.

Frequently, from the looks of it.

On the small landing at the top of the steps, a brown-

and-white mutt lifted its head at their approach, ears cocked, black nose twitching in their direction.

Fear sped her already-thrumming heart, followed immediately by a flash of annoyance. At what, specifically, she couldn't say. Her father, perhaps, for sending her here. Or Law, for having already thrown her off-kilter. Or the dog, for the memory it resurrected. All factors over which she had no control.

Not that she had control *issues*. Just overwhelming experience that life unfolded more smoothly when everything happened precisely according to her specifications 100 percent of the time.

Law cut the engine and swung out of his seat.

Marlowe followed suit somewhat more hesitantly, flinching when a whistle brought the dog bounding to his side, tail all a-swish with excitement.

She swung her satchel in front of her out of reflex, a move that drew his immediate attention.

"Layla, sit," he grunted.

All traces of nervous energy evaporated as the dog went completely still, parking its haunches on the ground and staring at him with adoration in its baleful eyes— one brown, one blue. As if it had been honored for the chance to obey.

If this was the sort of eager compliance Laurent Renaud was used to from all the females in his sphere, he was soon to be sincerely disappointed.

"Stay," he added.

Layla stayed.

Marlowe waited until Law had ascended the creaking stairs before following him, giving the dog a wide berth in the process.

A wall of cool, grain-scented air hit her full in the face as soon as she stepped through the door. The building was spacious, well organized and far cleaner than she had initially envisioned. Two rows of gleaming copper stills stretched out before her, a network of pipes extending from and between them. Beyond them, a maze of pallets stacked with cardboard boxes had been arranged into orderly rows, a forklift beeping as it drove its large metal tines beneath one of them.

"Up here." Law turned to a set of stairs leading to a loft with a gleaming wooden railing. She followed him up, pausing when she reached the landing.

Marlowe forced her face to remain stoic as she took in the sprawling chaos before her. A desk in the far corner, its surface heaped with piles of paper. An avalanche of folders spilling to the floor. A sad, sagging, imitation-leather couch with iron gray patches on the arms where countless elbows had buffed away the artificial taupe. Against the opposite wall, a boxy TV sat on a coffee table turned entertainment center—though the term felt nothing if not ironic in this context.

"Set up wherever." Standing in the small nook containing a sink, a coffee maker and an under-the-counter minifridge, Law twisted the tap demonstratively.

"Set up?" She blinked at him in confusion. "I assumed I'd be working directly with your accounting department."

"The accounting department is my brother Remy, and as you saw, he's occupied at the moment. The best I can do is log you in to his laptop." Bending over the desk closest to the stairs, Law tapped at the keyboard, then stood, granting her access. "Knock yourself out."

She looked from the laptop to Law, back to the laptop. "I know that 4 Thieves is a smaller operation than Kane Foods typically considers for investment, but as you're running a profitable business, I'm pretty sure you know that's actually not at all how this works."

Law closed the distance between them. His body appeared larger against this backdrop than it had with the sky as its only container. Despite her confidence-enhancing three-inch heels, he loomed over her, stone-faced and shirtless.

Dear God, *why* was he still shirtless?

She saw the fine splinters of wood in the dark chest hairs sprinkled over his pectoral muscles, narrowing into a dangerous trail that disappeared into the waist-band of his work pants beneath his taut belly button.

"What I know is that the only reason your father would send someone to conduct an on-site audit after everything we've already been through is so he could either continue to delay the process or remind me I'm at his mercy. Either way, I know he expects me to take one look at you, roll over and lap up whatever bullshit I'm fed." His eyes had darkened to the color of coffee left too long in the pot, as scorched and bitter as the words he spoke. "While I enjoy looking at you, you should know that I don't plan on spending any more time helping you to facilitate it than your father spent acknowledging my presence at his billionaire ball-tug."

As if the close air and his proximity hadn't been enough to steal her breath, his admission surely would have.

I enjoy looking at you...

Implying that he was both attracted to her and re-sented her for that attraction.

The realization spilled through her like molten honey

but failed to thaw the icy resentment at her center. Refusing to be cowed, she aimed her face into his glowering visage. "How do you propose I proceed, given those conditions?"

He cocked his head at an angle that would align their mouths in a perfect kiss if he were to lower his chin a mere four inches. "By reviewing the information that's been available to each of the third-party agencies who conducted the previous audits. All of it readily available in the folder labeled Audit on my brother's laptop," he said, sarcasm eating away at the edges of each word.

They stayed locked like this for an immeasurable stretch of time, drinking each other's exhalations, each unwilling to break.

"Ope! Sorry. Am I interrupting?" The voice was male, Midwestern and deepened by a pack-a-day nicotine croak.

Law looked away first, to Marlowe's great satisfaction.

"You're fine, Mike."

Mike, a stalky man with graying hair sprouting beneath a red trucker hat and a work shirt with his name embroidered on the pocket, shuffled to the printer stationed on Remy's desk. "I'm just here to grab the purchase orders for the Kentucky shipment. We're trying to get the trucks out before the storm."

"Storm?" A ripple of worry shimmered through Marlowe's stomach.

"Yes indeed, miss." Mike ducked his head deferentially. "Supposed to get hit hard by five o'clock. But you're perfectly safe here. This place is built like a bomb shelter. Should be out of our hair by tomorrow morning."

Shit.

She hadn't even bothered to check the weather before she'd left Philadelphia. Hadn't even booked a hotel room. Not that Fincastle had an abundance of options. She'd assumed she would be able to set out for her return voyage by early evening at the latest.

"Great," she said through gritted teeth.

Having retrieved his papers from the printer, Mike nodded to Law and loped down the stairs.

With exaggerated ceremony, Law took several steps backward, gripped the chair at Remy's desk and rolled it out in invitation. "Better get started."

And then, just as he had on the balcony of Fair Weather Hall, he turned and left.

"Are you a princess?"

Shoulders aching, neck stiff, eyes blurred from reviewing page after page of data, Marlowe looked up from the laptop screen to find a small, dark-haired girl with overlarge anime eyes gazing at her from the top of the stairs. In two small hands ending in nails with chipped, sparkly pink nail polish, she bore a silver tray.

"I'm a corporate-comptroller," Marlowe said, maintaining her posture in hopes of communicating she was in no hurry to be engaged in a lengthy conversation. She wasn't opposed to children as a general concept. Just preferred they existed *not* near her.

The small rosebud of a mouth tipped downward in a frown. "That sounds a lot less cool than a princess."

Marlowe glanced at her over her shoulder. "Princesses don't have a 401(k)."

"What's a 401(k)?" The girl scuffed forward on purple high-top shoes, lights blinking at the heels as she approached the desk.

Marlowe couldn't help but study every detail of this strange, small creature. The disheveled pigtail braids, too-large souvenir shop wolf-howling-at-the-moon T-shirt, iridescent rainbow leggings clinging to grasshopper-skinny legs.

"A 401(k) is a way you can take care of your future self."

With great care, the girl set the tray down. "Like with a time machine?" she asked.

"Kind of." Moved by the fantastical practicality of her logic, Marlowe smiled. "What's your name?"

"Emily." Her wide smile revealed a gummy gap where her two front teeth should be. "But Uncle Law calls me Bug."

"*Uncle* Law?" The idea that this little moppet could have any blood relation with the snarling, bare-chested barbarian of her recent acquaintance seemed completely incongruous.

The girl nodded. "He's really tall and he swears a lot but he's teaching me how to throw an axe."

Marlowe elected to let this new piece of information fly, despite her reservations. "Did Uncle Law also ask you to bring me a salad?"

"Actually—" Emily pronounced the word with exaggerated importance "—that was my dad. His name is Rainier but everyone calls him Remy. He's in charge of the restaurant."

"There's a restaurant?" Nothing she had yet seen in any of the financial information she had reviewed indicated an additional revenue source or the accompanying deductions.

The sound of boots thumping on the stairs sent a ripple of anticipation shivering through her, but the jolt she felt when she saw the dark head cresting the stairs snuffed out when the man's face came into view.

She recognized similarities in the slope of his jawline and arc in his cheekbones, the same way she could often pick out unknown pieces by a familiar composer. Variations on a theme.

"There you are," Remy said, casting a playfully censorious look in Emily's direction. "What did I tell you about bothering Miss Kane?"

Emily planted a hand on her narrow hip, her small face indignant. "I *wasn't* bothering her. I was just telling her about the restaurant."

"Did you tell her that you were supposed to be helping Mira finish rolling the silverware before the dinner shift?"

"I was totally going to, Dad," she huffed dramatically.

Holding his hand out, the man flashed Marlowe a smile. "Remy Renaud. It's a pleasure to meet you officially."

"Marlowe Kane," she said. "And thank you for sending my lunch. I hadn't realized how late it had gotten."

"Of course," Remy said. "You'll get to come out of the cave and join us for dinner, I hope?"

Glancing at the laptop, she felt her shoulders sag. "I was going to get in a few more hours, then head into town before the storm hits. I managed to grab a room at the Holiday Inn."

And she'd been lucky to get it. In the aftermath of

Law's tense exit, she had hopped on her phone and quickly discovered that the town's meager supply of hotels was selling out quickly as interstate travelers raced to get off the road.

"You're not staying here?" Remy asked.

"Where? In the office?" She flicked a worried look at the battered couch.

"We have a house on the property and several bungalows for staff, besides." His brows drew together as he cocked his head at a disbelieving angle. "Law really didn't mention this?"

"As it happens, he didn't."

Shaking his head, Remy sighed. "Manners never were his strong point."

"No argument there," she muttered under her breath.

"Tell you what." He snapped his fingers and clapped his hands together in a smooth cadence that led her to believe this was a frequently applied conversational transition. "You come down for dinner when you can, and I'll make sure something is set up for you. Deal?"

She considered, but only briefly. The idea of driving forty-five minutes into Roanoke and possibly during filthy weather appealed to her not at all. "Deal," she agreed.

Emily let out a little *whoop* and then caught herself.

Remy smiled indulgently. "All right, Em. Let's let this lady return to her work."

The girl retrieved her empty tray and propped it under her arm in a maneuver that looked oddly well practiced. "Enjoy your meal," she said.

When they dropped out of sight after the first set of stairs, Marlowe slumped into her chair.

Stuck overnight at 4 Thieves distillery with Law Renaud and a storm on the way.

What could possibly go wrong?

Four

"You realize that's the sixth time you've done that?" Grant Hutton asked in his annoyingly operatic voice.

Law paused with the damp rag in his hand, glancing at the already-pristine surface of the smooth mahogany bar top before turning to the man hefting a plastic crate of recently washed beer mugs to the counter.

With a full beard and a wild mane of russet hair that fell all the way to his shoulder blades when not contained in a man-bun, Grant had always reminded Law of a Viking. A Viking who had wandered into the twenty-first century and decided to trade his broadsword for lots of flannel and—when weather permitted—a Jeep.

Balling up the towel, Law shot it into a small stainless-steel sink filled with steaming bleach-laced water. "Your point?"

Grant dipped a red-knuckled hand into the crate and

began stacking the glasses on the shelf attached to the exposed brick wall behind the bar. "You just seem a little…distracted, is all."

He had been.

All that morning and for good stretches of the afternoon, he'd found himself staring off into the distance, his hands idle and his mind at work. Marlowe Kane might be stationed in the office, but she was still living rent free in his head.

There, he could watch her walk from her car in an endless loop, the muscles of her long, shapely legs tensing as she pretended not to struggle for footing on the gravel. More memorable still, the hard, hungry look she hadn't quite managed to hide before returning her face to its mask of calculated calm.

True, he'd loaded the deck.

Making sure he had been both shirtless and chopping wood when she arrived might have been a shade underhanded, but it had also proved marvelously effective.

As had the load of scrap metal Remy had "accidentally" dropped on the road to the distillery. Their brief, wild ATV ride had been the most action he'd had in he couldn't even remember how long. Hours later, he could still feel the ghost of her hand on his thigh, mere inches from his cock.

In his mind, it didn't stay there.

"So, when do we get to meet her?" This new voice, husky and gently mocking, belonged to Mira Reyes. A full foot shorter than Law but arguably just as tough, she had short, ink-black hair and a take-no-shit temperament. A problem, considering how likely he and Remy were to give it.

The Blackpot's dining-room manager, she'd worked

a handful of jobs in the distillery warehouse and had the biceps to prove it.

Shouldering past Grant, she dumped a bucket of ice nearly as tall as she was into the bar's cooler. "And don't bother saying 'meet who?' Remy told us *all* about her."

Because of course he did.

"She's here to do an audit." Law reached into the fridge and pulled out a beer, popping the cap off on the edge of the counter. "Not to play homecoming queen of 4 Thieves."

Mira placed a hand on her hip, her dark eyes fixed on the bottle cap he'd let fall to the floor.

On a grousing sigh, Law bent to pick it up, then dropped it in the trash.

"She's coming to dinner!" The high, clear bell of Emily's voice rang through the still-empty restaurant. She galloped past the hostess station and twirled, the frilly skirt of her favorite princess dress flaring out around her slight frame.

"Is that right?" Mira slung the bucket onto her shoulder.

"Yes!" His niece practically sang. "Dad invited her. Oh, Mira, she's *so* pretty and she has blond hair, and just *wait* till you see her shoes."

Grant came up beside Law, polishing one of the beer mugs that apparently hadn't passed muster. "What were you saying about that homecoming-queen thing?" he asked, loud enough to be heard by residents of the next county.

Lifting the beer to his lips, Law took a greedy pull. "Shut up. Everything ready in the kitchen?"

"Has it ever not been?" Mira arched a scornful eyebrow at him. "Although, I don't even know why we're bothering. With this storm coming, I bet we don't get even ten people tonight."

Law knew she was likely right but wouldn't give her the satisfaction of saying so. He crossed to the end of the bar and stepped out, unable to stanch the swell of pride. The restaurant had been an unintended addition to their original plan. What had started as locals showing up to buy direct had turned into tours. Then out-of-town groups wanting to come sample had ended up staying. Remy, who had been just as obsessed about perfecting the art of smoking meat as he had distilling spirits, would offer dinner, and before long, Blackpot had become a staple.

The ragtag staff of 4 Thieves had been assembled just as organically. People who had wandered into their realm from varying walks of life and committed their hearts and souls to a dream that hadn't even been theirs.

What began as a business now felt like a family. Dysfunctional though it may be sometimes.

"She's here!" Emily shot from her seat at the table and bounded toward the hostess stand, where Marlowe stood, surveying the space. Despite her wind-mussed hair and rumpled blouse—details that made Law's ever-suspicious antennae twitch—she looked every bit as fresh and lovely as she had that morning.

He noted that with great displeasure.

Remy's arrival only seconds later did nothing to lift his darkening mood. He'd donned a shirt with actual sleeves for the occasion, but his hair bore all the hallmarks of a quick jaunt on his much-beloved Harley.

The image of Marlowe clutching his brother from behind while tearing down the country roads charred Law's insides like so much napalm.

"Dad!" Emily said, practically bouncing foot to foot. "Can I give her a tour?"

"If Miss Kane wants to and your uncle Law doesn't mind," Remy said.

Encouraged by his brother's use of *Miss* and wanting the chance to grill him privately, Law looked to his niece. "Knock yourself out."

"Yay!" Grabbing Marlowe by the hand, Emily nearly pulled her off her heels. "This way. I'll show you the barrel room and the axe gallery and…" The list eventually faded away as they disappeared through the doorway.

Mira and Grant suddenly remembered urgent tasks that needed completing and disappeared through the swinging door to the kitchen.

Remy ran a hand through his hair as he walked to the bar and helped himself to a beer. "Getting pretty dirty out there."

Lifting his own beer, Law took a steadying sip. "Where were you two coming from?"

"What makes you think we were coming from the same place?" His brother tipped back the brown bottle, his stubble-flecked Adam's apple bobbing as he swallowed.

"Because you two arrived together and she sure looks like she's been riding *something*," Law said.

"Your ass would be my guess." Remy set the beer on the bar and wiped the sweat from his face with a paper towel. "She hasn't left the office all day."

"And how would you know?"

"Because I can see the outside door from the goddamn pile of scrap metal *you* had me drop," Remy said, raking a hand through his disheveled hair. "Unless she's been hanging out in the mash house or shipping dock, I'm guessing she just stayed put."

Feeling slightly sheepish, Law picked at the label on his beer.

"While we're on the subject, you want to tell me why that was necessary?" his brother asked. "Because I know it wasn't just so you could cart her here in the Varmint."

That was where his brother was wrong.

He'd wanted to get Marlowe as close to him as he could get her without making his intentions overtly obvious. His brother's Frankenstein of an all-terrain vehicle just happened to be the perfect excuse. If he was being forced to endure this farce of an audit, he intended to enjoy it as much as possible.

"Just want to make sure she gets the full 4 Thieves experience," Law drawled, downing another swallow.

Remy shook his head. "That, or you're pulling her pigtails like a grade school bully."

There may have been a shade more truth in the accusation than Law wanted to admit.

"And *this* is where people can buy bottles directly if they want to take anything home with them. Bourbon, whiskey, vodka and gin." Emily held her hand out with the exaggerated importance of a model showing off an '80s game show prize.

They had made the full loop and now stood opposite the wooden mailroom-box grid they'd repurposed into shelving for their various spirits.

"Personally, I would recommend the bourbon. Ours is triple distilled and has notes of maple and toasted pecans," she continued importantly.

Marlowe glanced across the room at Law and Remy,

a look of bemused concern on her face. "Please tell me this child is not speaking from experience."

Setting his beer aside, Law strolled over to them. "Only a sip for tasting purposes. We're going to wait until she's at least twelve to move on to shots."

"Uncle *Law*," his niece groaned, turning to look beseechingly at Marlowe. "He's only kidding. I've never actually tried anything. I just heard a lot of people say those things."

Emily blinked at their guest with giant, hopeful eyes. "You're still staying for dinner, right?"

"I guess that depends." Marlowe looked around quizzically at the completely empty dining room. "You think they could find us a table?"

Quickly picking up on the humor, his niece's lips stretched into a smile.

Law silently willed her to choose a table. Preferably one in the center with at least six chairs so he had plenty of room to spread out.

Apparently, his subliminal skills were severely lacking.

Emily made a beeline straight for a booth with windows overlooking the rolling hills, shadowed beneath a darkening carpet of gray. She quickly doled out the menus while providing the marching orders.

"Daddy and Uncle Law, you sit on this side, and then we can sit across from you."

"Ladies first," Law said, barring Remy with an arm so he could decide whether to slide in first or second.

"You go ahead," Emily urged Marlowe. "Just in case I need to help if more people come."

"She takes her hostess duties very seriously," Remy

explained, squeezing Emily's shoulder through the puffy sleeve of her dress.

"I can see that." Marlowe complied with his niece's request, scooting into the booth. After Emily had followed, Law slid in before his brother, doing his worst-best to keep his knees from brushing Marlowe's under the table.

Grant appeared shortly thereafter and took their drink orders.

Emily, looking somewhat concerned that Marlowe wasn't going to try any of the drinks featuring their house spirits, seemed mollified when she promised to buy a bottle to take back to Philadelphia.

What followed may have been the most torturous forty-seven minutes of Law's life.

Mira had been right.

Their small party had been the restaurant's only patrons that evening.

Law sat watching Marlowe take small, polite bites of the smoked turkey breast and side salad she had ordered while patiently answering each of Emily's approximately seven thousand questions. He wondered if this was a skill unique to the truly wealthy: the ability to consume a meal so inconspicuously that conversation seemed like the more important activity.

He wondered if she even tasted her food. Whether she'd ever eaten something truly indulgent just for the pleasure of it.

When a spear of lightning silvered the darkened landscape, Remy caught Law's eye, tapped the table and leaned toward his daughter. "All right. Bedtime, Barbara Walters."

"Who even is that?" Emily scraped the last bit of

muddy hot fudge from the dish of ice cream Grant had brought out for her after everyone else had declined dessert.

"Someone your dad is old enough to remember." Remy slid out of the booth, stretched and held out a hand to his daughter. "You want to tell the kitchen they can go ahead and close down early?"

Her eyes widened at the prospect, this kind of official duty perhaps the only thing capable of tearing her away from the elegant city princess before her. "Absolutely," she said, pausing to lift her napkin and delicately dab the corners of her mouth. A gesture so obviously stolen from Marlowe that he had to suppress a chuckle.

They went through a standard round of have-a-good-nights and see-you-tomorrows.

Then they were alone.

Marlowe rolled the stem of her chardonnay glass between two fingers, a pensive look on her face. "Where's her mother?"

Piqued at her directness, Law sipped at his whiskey, relishing the burn as it slid down his throat. "She and Remy hadn't been together very long when she got pregnant. They decided to make a go of it. Got married in a hurry. Got divorced just as fast. She stuck around for about six months after the birth, then went to visit friends and never returned."

Marlowe looked up from her wine, eyes almost aqua as they reflected the golden glow from the lamp overhead. "I just don't understand how anyone could do that."

Law had spent his whole life trying.

"Some people just weren't meant to be parents," he

said. Having a father like his, this was as close as he had ever come to any kind of answer.

A shadow passed over her features, tightening her lips. "I can't argue with that assessment."

Never one to press for personal details, Law stayed silent, leaving space she could speak into, should she want it.

"Does Emily ever ask about her?"

Noticing Marlowe's glass was empty, Law reached for the bottle Grant had left on the table before checking out for the night. He held it up in question and was met with a nod.

"She used to," Law said, pouring the wine. "Even wrote her a letter once."

Marlowe raised a hand to signal "enough." "Did her mother respond?"

Law set the bottle aside and took a fortifying swallow of his own drink. "Came back unopened."

Her delicate tawny brows drew together, her lovely, wine-wet mouth hovering slightly open.

And God, what that wounded look did to him.

He was seized by the overpowering urge to lean across the table and chase the pain away. With his lips. With his hands. With his body.

Then her expression quickly shifted, replaced by one that inflamed him even more.

Anger, pure and powerful, flushed her cheeks, crimsoned her lips, hardened her irises into glittering diamonds. The look that had reached all the way across the crowded grand-entry hall slid straight down his pants and wrapped its fist firmly around his cock.

To discover the full depths of the volcanic heat trapped beneath her icy demeanor. To let it scald and seduce him.

He wanted this.

He wanted *her*.

"How anyone could do something so cruel to such a sweet, smart, beautiful little girl…" She drained the meager amount she'd allowed him to pour in one swallow and set the glass down so hard the stem broke.

And with it, the brief display of her temper.

"I—I'm so sorry," she stammered.

"Don't be." He caught her hand as she reached for the broken glass. "Let me. Can't comb through data with your hands sliced to ribbons," he teased, to cut the tension thickening the air around them.

After wrapping the glass bowl and stem in a cloth napkin, he found a small cardboard box in the kitchen and labeled it before putting it in the trash. He stopped behind the bar to grab a bottle of whiskey and a second glass before returning to the table.

She regarded him warily as he approached. "What, may I ask, do you propose to do with that?"

"Ruin you for all other whiskeys." Rain lashed at the window as Law peeled the wax seal from the cap and pulled the cork out with a friendly squeak. He poured them each two fingers and slid one of the glasses over to her.

"I'm not in the habit of drinking it neat," she said, eyeing it dubiously.

"I don't want you to drink it. I want you to *taste* it," he said. "Sipped neat, the warmth of your mouth will open up the more subtle flavors. But if it's too strong for you…"

"Please," she scoffed. "I'm the product of WASP DNA. My liver could process rocket fuel."

Law felt the liquor beginning to work. Warming

his chest, loosening his joints. "My father would have loved you."

"Was he a rocket scientist?" Her lips curled in a sexy smirk that sent warmth pooling in other, more problematic areas.

"More like an unattended scrap-metal acquisition specialist and purveyor of craft spirits. Moonshine being one of them."

"I thought most of that ceased with the end of Prohibition." Marlowe reached for her drink and held it just below her nose, her nostrils flaring as she inhaled. When she brought it to her lips, he couldn't help but mentally trace the path it would follow. Over her tongue, down the smooth column of her neck, into her belly.

"Zap Renaud wasn't one to let laws get in the way of a business opportunity. He was kind of a legend around Terrebonne Parish. And not in a good way."

"Zap?" she repeated.

"Before he started 'shining, he was a remarkably mediocre electrician. An unfortunate accident led to his change in career paths." Law snugged the cork in the bottle and picked it up from the table. "That's about when he started having us go on 'missions.'"

"Are you positive he wasn't a rocket scientist?" she asked.

"Unless rocket scientists routinely have their teenage sons steal scrap metal and other items needed to build a still."

"Right." He could tell by the sparkle in her eye that she thought he was kidding. When she saw that he wasn't, it abruptly winked out. "He really made you do that?"

"More like made it undesirable not to."

Their father's means had been vast, varied, frequently

requiring cooperation and stealth that left them hissing at each other under their breath.

"I'm sorry," Marlowe said.

"Don't be," Law replied. "Come with me."

"Where?" she asked, her voice laced with a smoky depth from the whiskey.

"You'll see." He took a few slow steps backward and was gratified when she scooted to the end of the bench and stood.

"You forget I've had the official tour. I've seen everything there is to see."

Hand on her hip, she cocked her head at the arrogant angle that simultaneously irked and aroused him.

"It's not something I want you to see," he said, aware of the desire darkening his tone. "It's something I want you to do."

Five

"You've got to be kidding me." Odd, how many times Marlowe had uttered this phrase in one day. She stood before a stall bordered by a chain-link fence that stretched from the floor to the lowered ceilings on either side. At the end of the makeshift gallery, the large, round lid of an old whiskey barrel hung on the wall, a target painted on its surface.

In the center of the target was an axe.

"You don't strike me as the type who's big on the jokes." The muscles of Law's broad shoulders flexed through the fabric of his shirt—thank God he was wearing one—as he jerked the axe free of the wood. He walked to her with slow, measured strides and placed the wicked-looking tool on a table that bore several others of varying size and shape.

"What part of hurling dangerous projectiles after

consuming alcoholic beverages *doesn't* strike you as a bad idea?" She gestured to the bottle of whiskey that sat adjacent to the axes like a visual advertisement for disastrous choices.

"A tool is only dangerous in the hands of someone who doesn't know how to use it properly."

Marlowe raised her non-drink-bearing hand. "Yeah. Hi. That's me. I don't know how to use an axe properly."

Law set his drink on the table next to the bottle. "That's why I'm going to teach you."

A delicate flutter rippled through her whiskey-warmed middle. "Why would I want to learn something that will have absolutely no practical application in my everyday life?"

Law's lips tilted in a smirk as he reached for the nearest axe. "I said the same thing about quadratic functions in high school, and yet here we are, about to calculate some trajectories."

Marlowe blinked at him, stunned mute. Of all the reasons she had expected him to provide her, this had surely not been one of them.

"How about this?" he continued when she failed to respond. "You need to blow off some steam, and I have a finite amount of stemware."

Marlowe sipped the whiskey and set aside her glass, knowing it was a painfully obvious attempt to disprove his assessment. "Please, O wielder of hardware, teach me this most sacred of manly arts that will miraculously dispel my visibly apparent tension."

The heated way he looked at her mouth when she'd finished saying this caused a fine sheen of sweat to bloom on the back of her neck.

He came around the table and stood dead center of

the stall about twelve feet away from the target, turning to crook two fingers at her.

Something about the way his roughened fingertips curled in an invitation sent a shower of sparks shimmering through her.

On a bratty sigh, she acquiesced.

"You're going to need to lose the shoes," he said, glancing at her heels.

Though the idea of adding several inches to the already-significant height gap between them didn't thrill her, the prospect of her bare feet on the cool cement floor wasn't exactly unpleasant.

She stepped out of them, dropping the top of her head to about his chin level. A smile flickered across his lips.

"Now one foot slightly forward." He stepped one large work boot out, waiting until she begrudgingly mimicked his stance.

Holding the axe by the blunt end of the head, he angled the handle toward her. "I'm assuming you've played golf?"

Marlowe took it, wrapping her right hand around its base in a classic golf-club grip. "You're assuming a lot of things, it seems."

Without a word, he released his demonstrative posture and stalked behind her with a predatory efficiency of movement. Awareness crackled around her, electrifying the air. It was as if the molecules displaced by his body bore the memory of him as they moved over her skin.

"May I?"

These two words spoken in his deep, resonant voice made gooseflesh rise on her arms. Whether it was the whiskey, or the storm, or the wildness of being free from supervising eyes, she felt far enough from the cautious prison of her mind to answer without hesitation.

"You may."

She sensed him. The wall of his chest close but not touching, the abdominal muscles she'd seen exposed earlier a hairbreadth from her spine.

And she felt him.

His hand covered hers and guided it up the smooth wood before capturing her left and lifting it, molding it to the handle just below her right.

Marlowe's heart was a drum played with wild abandon, her blood quickly becoming devoid of oxygen because she'd forgotten how to breathe.

"Good," he rumbled from behind her. "Loosen your grip. You're trying to throw it, not choke it."

Was it purely her imagination, or had the word *choke* received particular attention?

With great effort, she relaxed her fingers slightly.

"Yes, just like that." His breath tickled her neck as his hands hovered over hers once more, his arms warm, smooth and hard as they folded in. "Next, you're going to lift until the head of the axe comes all the way over your shoulder."

Lifting together, he helped her bring the axe back as far as his body would allow.

"Rock your hips forward, follow with your torso and let the motion move all the way through your arms."

The ridges of his hip bones nudged her lower back as his torso melted against hers. He moved their bodies in a slow, sensual undulation that sent what little moisture remained in Marlowe's mouth straight to her panties.

Hard as she tried, she couldn't detect the telltale bulge where she calculated it should be if he felt even a fraction of the heady, drugging arousal tingling through her limbs.

Not that this offended her.

Much.

Just when she thought she would either die or burst into flames spontaneously, Law brought their combined limbs back over their heads and paused when the axe was eye level. "Release when the handle is directly in front of your face."

Marlowe nodded, grappling to keep her concentration despite the vivid mental imagery of a completely different kind of release.

"Ready?" he asked.

God, was she. The question vibrated from his chest through her back, causing her nipples to harden deliciously against the cups of her utilitarian bra.

"Yes," she said.

He stepped to the side, and she lifted her arms, surprised how much heavier the axe felt when not partially borne by his strength.

"Final tip," he said, followed by the squeak of the cork and the sound of him refilling their glasses. "Keep your eyes on where you want the axe to go. Bonus points if you picture the face of someone who's pissed you off."

"Someone *other* than you, you mean?" she asked, only half teasing.

"Marlowe Kane," he drawled, "you can split me in half if it pleases you."

At that precise moment, what she wanted was quite the opposite. Letting her lids fall closed, she drew in a long, deep inhalation, conjuring the face of every man who had ever spoken down to her, leered at her, took credit for her ideas, cooed at her like some kind of pet. Neil, her father and countless others. Balling them into one smug composite, she let the electric charge of rage build in her belly and spread until her entire being hummed like the live end of a downed power line.

Her body took over, rocking back, then forward as her arms swung like the beam of a trebuchet. She watched the axe fly, somersaulting through the air until the blade bit into the barrel lid with a satisfying thump, just right of the round, red bull's-eye.

The sweet, purging fire of adrenaline sang in her veins, and before she even knew what she was doing, she'd picked up another axe, then another and another, until every last one was buried in the wood. Marlowe hadn't even realized she'd made a sound until she heard the guttural echoes still bouncing from the corrugated walls and wood beams.

She turned to find Law standing there frozen, the glass of whiskey halfway to his open mouth. Such a sight she must be, barefoot and panting, her cheeks burning, her nipples forming darts beneath the thin fabric of her blouse.

Law cleared his throat, resuming his composure but not quite managing to keep his eyes from her breasts as she padded over to him. "You're—" His voice broke, and he coughed before resuming. "You're supposed to get your axe after each throw."

Marlowe retrieved her glass and took a sip, relishing how the smoky, silky burn tangled with the metallic sharpness on her tongue. "You didn't tell me that."

"If you hit another axe, the metal can sliver and ricochet. Or splinters from the handle could hit someone." Once again, his dark eyes made an abrupt but distinctly un-stealthy pilgrimage downward.

She glanced at the barrel target with its not-exactly-neat-but-not-entirely-chaotic circle of axes. "Good thing I didn't do that, isn't it?"

Thunder rattled the rafters as the downpour intensified, roaring on the distillery's roof. That primal rush seemed to sink into her, meeting the pounding of her pulse, which had found its way to the sweet ache building between her thighs.

Keeping her gaze on Law's, she dipped a finger into the whiskey and brought it to her lips, feeling them molten beneath the pad of her fingertip.

His eyelids lowered, his irises warming to a rich sienna. When he spoke, his words were raspy and low. "What are you doing?"

She took a step closer, allowing her breasts to brush his arm. "Didn't you say warmth enhanced the flavor?"

His knuckles whitened as he gripped his drink. "This feels like a decision you're going to regret."

Marlowe hooked a finger around the metal buckle of his belt and pulled his hips toward her belly, knowing that she could say what needed saying. Only tonight. Only here. Only with him.

"I like looking at you too, Law. I like your hands, and I like your mouth, and I want to feel them on me. I've wanted it since the first time I saw you at Fair Weather Hall. As for regrets, I'd rather regret having you than regret leaving here tomorrow and never knowing what it might have been like. I recognize that might not be the case for you. I accept that. But now you know where I stand."

Only, she wasn't standing.

Not anymore.

His hands were on her hips, lifting her easily, setting her on the raised table where the axes had been and the whiskey and their glasses still were. The resulting configuration brought her much closer to his height.

A fact she became acutely aware of as his face came nearer to hers than it had ever been. Near enough for her to see the scattered copper threads around pupils as dark and tempest-tossed as the night.

"Where?" he grunted.

Marlowe resisted the urge to look away. "Where *what*?"

He leaned in until she could feel the warmth from his lips through the thin scrim of air that separated them. "*Where* do you want my mouth?"

"Wherever you want to—"

"No." The sound was little more than a growl. "That night, on the balcony, your jackass of a fiancé told *you* what turned you on. You're going to tell *me*, or this is as far as we go."

Of all the things to demand from her.

How could she possibly put into words what turned her on? She was already so turned on just by his presence that the part of her brain dedicated to speech had popped like a blown circuit.

Law pulled away slightly, sensing her indecision.

With great care, he ran the rough pad of his thumb over her lower lip. "Here?" he asked. "Was that why you put the whiskey on your lips? You wanted me to taste it on you?"

She nodded eagerly, grateful to be read.

Correctly, for once.

Law reached behind her, picked up his glass and took a sip. Cupping her jaw in the safe nest of his two palms, he told her with his eyes what he couldn't with his mouth.

She closed the infinitesimal gap between them, her lips soft and slightly parted.

Together they melted in a shared sip of smoky sweetness as Law let the liquor trickle from his mouth to hers, only to drink it again from her with the slow, thorough strokes of his tongue. So lost in the moment, it took Marlowe the space of unknown seconds to remember she could kiss him back.

Hesitantly at first, she joined the dance, allowing her tongue to roll and glide, to flick and stroke in time with his. Encouraged by his groan, she threaded her fingers into the dark, silky tendrils at the base of his neck, marveling at the decadence of this sensation. Never once in her twenty-nine years had Marlowe been with a man whose hair was long enough to handle this way.

"Where else?" he mumbled, their ragged breath mingling.

Hands still in his hair, she exposed her throat and gently pulled him toward it. He wasted no time trailing kisses down her jawline, pausing to lick and suck places made deliciously sensitive by the stubble of his chin. When he reached her earlobe, Marlowe shuddered, surprised to feel him cradle her nape when her head fell backward in helpless pleasure.

There he stayed for time without end, not as a brief stop on the way to somewhere else but to fully explore every dip and hollow until she couldn't keep from squirming with impatience.

Law lifted his head, his hooded eyes focused and intent. He traced her clavicle with the tip of his finger, following the dip at the base of her throat, then downward, stopping when he met the fabric of her blouse. "Next?"

Had Marlowe not remembered she didn't have a change of clothes, she might have torn open her shirt in a scatter of buttons. Presently, she wouldn't even trust her hands not to shake enough to undo them herself. Luckily, Law seemed more than obliged, quickly flicking them open one-handed.

She helped him by shrugging out of the sleeves, leaving only her bra, skirt and already-soaked panties to be dealt with.

"Not so fast," he said, gently foiling her as she reached for the clasp on her bra.

Laurent Renaud wasn't a man to be hurried.

Only after he had extended his exploration to the curve of her shoulder did he thumb the straps down, reach for the hooks at her back and peel the bra away.

Here, he paused his ministrations, gazing at her with rapt attention.

Apprehension tightened her stomach.

Marlowe had always been self-conscious of her breasts, which she felt were small, the nipples too large, and all of it somehow out of kilter with her angular hips and too-wide shoulders. She'd been hoping to fast-forward through this part, as she always had with Neil, who had seemed happy to let her.

"How are you real?" Reverently, he trailed his knuckles along her sternum and outward across her rib cage, looping up and around, only to repeat it on the opposite side. A maddening figure eight that made her burn for his touch until he, at last, brought his mouth to one rosy peak. With the tip of his tongue, he circled her nipple, flicking the taut pearl before testing it with his teeth.

Pleasure flashed from her breast straight through her core, a sensory reflection of the lightning arcing across the sky outside, seeking ground. Her back arched, pushing into his mouth, greedy, gluttonous. Just when she thought this sensation alone might send her over the edge, Law moved to her other breast, building the fire anew.

She became aware of her small, bleating cries of demand, and then he was moving again, finding her mouth. They devoured each other, dueling as their minds and words had since the moment they had met, each spurring the other on to bolder and hungrier volleys twice as intoxicating as the whiskey they tasted of.

Marlowe clawed at the edge of his soft, well-worn T-shirt, dragging it over his head and tossing it aside before widening her knees and hooking her ankles around his calves. Law helped. Eager hands pushed her skirt around her hips, cupping her ass and dragging her to the very edge of the table, where the crotch of her soaked panties met his steely arousal through the fabric of his work pants.

She whimpered into his mouth, undulating her hips to intensify the delicious friction. Already, she felt the first heady contractions.

With a wicked grin teasing his kiss-swollen lips, he eased her torso backward until the exposed skin of her back came into contact with the cool, smooth surface of the wood.

"I wish you could see yourself." His warm, heavy hand came to rest over her wildly beating heart. "You're so fucking beautiful like this."

"Like what?" she asked breathlessly.

Lifting the hand from her chest, he reached beyond

her shoulder and dipped his finger in his abandoned glass. With an amber droplet hanging from his finger like a glittering topaz, he painted a line from her belly button to her black panties.

"Undone." His powerful torso folded over her, hands gripping her hips through the bunched fabric of her skirt as he planted kisses down the gleaming trail, slipping his tongue beneath the waistband of her underwear. He then retraced his steps, rubbing his cheek and jaw over skin made sensitive by his lips and tongue.

Her stomach shuddered as chills broke out from her scalp to her curling toes. This seemed to please Law, who looked at her through a fringe of obscenely long eyelashes bleached golden at the tips from long days under the late-summer sun.

Propping herself up on her elbows, Marlowe watched as he drew her panties down her legs before sinking to his knees. There, he continued his maddeningly deliberate onslaught. Kissing, licking, sucking and sampling the skin of her inner thighs, gently abrading it with his jaw. What his mouth didn't touch, his hands did. Or his chest. His stomach. His hips.

Constant contact. His need to taste her, to breathe her and feel her.

All of her.

As if her entire body were an extension of the parts of her that previous partners had always immediately gravitated toward. As if Law knew her sex could be teased from the backs of her knees, the dimple above her hip, a shadowed notch outside her elbow.

Used to living on her own 99.9 percent of the time, Marlowe had never spent much thought on her own body, save to provide it with exercise, hydration and adequate nutrition.

And here he was, making her *aware* of herself. Making her feel alive in ways she hadn't known possible until this night, under his hands. Not as a being of purpose but as a creature of pleasure. Capable of existing on passion improbably sweet as clover honey and ephemeral as a summer storm.

By the time his lips grazed the juncture at the apex of her thighs, he had honed her to such a fevered pitch that she almost tumbled over the cliff right then and there.

Seeing the way her torso had jerked, Law raised an eyebrow at her. "Trying to end my fun so soon?"

"*Your* fun?" Bare breasts overrun with a riotous flush rose and fell in time with her uneven breaths.

"Make no mistake." He kissed a freckle on the inside of her thigh. "Getting you wet is my favorite part."

As if to confirm just how well he'd accomplished this, he slid his fingers up and down her slippery folds.

"Oh, *baby*," he groaned appreciatively, delving deeper.

This alone might have sent her into orbit after a very short countdown had it not been for his sublimely rough, beautifully tapered, blunt-ended thumb. It had barely brushed the sensitive bud at the crest of her sex when her entire body seized. Racked by wave after wave, she surrendered any pretext of decorum or self-control, dissolving into shivering convulsions narrated with the yowl of a feral cat.

Law held her shaking legs, his face breaking into bemused appreciation when the tremors began to quiet. "Not bad," he said. "But I think I can do better."

"Do…better?" Though Marlowe felt like a marionette whose strings had been cut, she managed to lift her head.

"You didn't think I was done, did you?" His hands found the creases where her thighs met her hips, the skin in and around them already beginning to tingle again.

"Yes," she said too quickly. "I mean, no. I mean, I thought we would—"

"Oh, we will." He skimmed his palms down her legs until they'd reached her knees, drawn together during her mild seizure. Keeping his eyes on hers, he eased them open to the width of his broad shoulders. "But not until I've made you come at least seven times."

"S-seven?" she stammered. Thunder rolled in the distance, strangely appropriate punctuation for the prospect she now faced.

"One for every axe you threw." Leaning forward, he captured both nipples between his thumbs and forefingers and began to roll them slowly. "Also, seven happens to be my lucky number."

Marlowe opened her mouth to protest, but then his tongue split her while his hands set to work, and try as she might, she couldn't remember why she had ever thought this was a bad idea.

Six

Law cursed himself for the worst kind of idiot.

The more times he watched Marlowe Kane coming apart, the direr his need to *feel* her do it around his cock. They'd gotten as far as five when, looking at her sweat-slicked breasts, he could no longer bear the strangled tightness of his work pants.

He paused only to unbuckle his belt but was preempted by Marlowe, who quickly sat and tore at the button and zipper with shaking hands.

The closest thing to hunger he'd seen her express.

After having watched the careful, self-controlled way she ate, he'd wondered if she ever let anyone feed her. Body or soul.

Judging by her reaction to their encounter thus far, he suspected he had his answer. There were plenty of notches in his bedpost, but Law couldn't think of a single time a woman had been so responsive to, so appreciative of, the most basic level of physical contact.

Were he not completely engulfed in a firestorm of lust, he would be tempted to hop in his truck and drive the five hours to Philadelphia just to have a little conversation with Neil.

To be trusted by a woman this beautiful, this passionate, and leave her touch-starved and unsatisfied was an unforgivable offense in his book.

Not that he was any less ravenous.

It had been over a year since Jessica left, and things had cooled considerably between them physically long before that.

Law's teeth clenched, and he banished the memory, determined to stay in the moment. To enjoy this one, good thing as long as it lasted.

Or as long as *he* lasted.

Feeling her hand slide along his entire erect length, he knew he was in imminent danger of losing himself as quickly as she had. He quickly jerked his hips back, mildly touched by the petulant look on Marlowe's features. Disappointed to have an item of interest taken away from her.

"So, you can touch me as much as you like, but your equipment is off-limits?" she asked.

"Equipment?" Law leaned against the table to reach down and untie his boots, kicking off one and then the other before stripping off his socks. "Is that drawing-room etiquette, or do you just have an aversion to anatomical terms?"

She sat a little straighter. How she managed to look haughtily offended while topless and with her skirt bunched around her hips beat the hell out of him.

"I don't have an aversion to anything. I was just pointing out the inequity in the rules of engagement." The acerbic, calculating part of her brain that a handful of orgasms had temporarily shorted seemed to be once again firing at full throttle.

"It makes me crazy when you talk like that." He pushed his work pants to his ankles and stepped out of them, leaving only boxer briefs that did absolutely nothing to conceal his painfully hard erection.

Her eyes skimmed downward, her mouth widening a fraction before flattening into an irritable line.

"You want to take them off?" he asked, stepping forward as an offering.

Marlowe folded her arms over her naked breasts.

"Fair is fair, right?" he teased.

Something in her manner changed then, her pupils dilating, eyes softening. "No," she said. "I want to watch."

This phrase, spoken in the husky tone of a silver-screen starlet, tossed gasoline on the flames licking at his groin. With fingers in the waistband of his boxers, he drew them down slowly, deliberately, until he stood naked before her.

Her gaze fixed on the part of him standing hot and hard at attention as she bit her lower lip. Then her expression shifted again, and cocking her head at an imperious angle, she looked at him down the length of her elegant nose.

"Are you going to come do something about that?" She lazily ran her long, lovely fingers over the small, downy patch between her legs.

The combination of the deliberately provocative visual with her haughty, overbred diction was dynamite in the dam of his self-restraint. He closed the distance between them in two strides, grabbed her by the backs of her knees and scooted her to the edge of the table.

"Sit up," he said. "You wanted to watch, and you're going to watch."

She pushed herself up on her palms. Her cheeks flushed atomic pink as her eyes nervously darted to his face. "I don't really—"

Law shifted his hips forward, relishing her small cry as he coated the head of his cock in her ample moisture and grazed her taut, slick bud. He repeated the motion again. Then again. And again, until her hips began to move in concert.

"*This* is what it looks like when you're turned on," he said. "If a man doesn't do this to you, he doesn't deserve the honor of your body."

"Please," she whispered.

"I said seven. I meant seven."

Her legs jerked. Fingers clenched on the edge of the table, she began to writhe and squirm. What began as whispering gasps and panting breaths were building to lush, urgent grunts and silky moans. Quickening the slippery side-to-side motion, he watched as the flat plane of her belly began to quake.

"That's it, sugar," he urged.

Her torso lurched on a startled sob. She clutched his forearms as a hot, wet gush bathed him.

Marlowe's already-flushed cheeks darkened to a beet red. "I'm not—" she stammered. "I've never—"

"Now you have." He leaned forward and brushed her lips with his. "And not for the last time, if I have my say."

Their kiss turned hungry. Demanding. Her hands were everywhere. Gripping his hair, gliding over the slopes of his shoulders, palming his pectoral muscles and moving over his stomach.

"Please," she said again, pulling her face away from his to whisper hot words in his ear. "I want to feel you."

Engulfed as he was, a sharp pang of regret pierced him. "I don't have anything with me." In fact, he hadn't needed them in so long that he wasn't even positive the foil packets at the bottom of his sock drawer were even there.

Marlowe palmed his ass and undulated her hips to slide against his length. "I'm on birth control."

Relief evicted the regret until he remembered *who* she had been on birth control for. The need to drive the memory of every man she'd ever been with and those she'd only just thought about blazed through him like wildfire. "You're sure?" he asked.

"Positive." She looked at him with eyes half-obscured with lowered lids, her kiss-swollen lips curved by a sensual smile. Her smooth, warm leg folded around his, the bottom of her foot planted on the back of his calf.

This small, affectionate gesture released a tide of warmth in his chest. Law couldn't remember the last time he'd felt this.

Wanted.

But wanted by a woman like Marlowe Kane?

Never in his thirty-four years.

He stroked the outside of her thigh from hip to knee and, when he'd reached it, lifted her leg and hooked it over the crook of his elbow. Slowly, he leaned forward until he could plant the same hand on the table, leaving his other free to…explore.

And he did.

Beginning at her jaw, he memorized the lines of her

body the way a blind man might, imprinting upon his palm the width and curve of her neck, the swell of her breast, the rippled terrain of her ribs, the subtle outcropping of her hip, the rising mound of her sex.

When he reached it, he gently pushed the heel of his hand against the soft flesh just above the bony ridge, earning himself a cagey look.

"Trust me," he said.

An unreasonable request to make, save for this present moment.

Law hissed a breath through his teeth as he slowly sank into her velvet depths, stopping abruptly when her mouth twitched in a slight grimace.

"You okay?" he asked, the primal rushing of his heartbeat nearly drowning out the downpour.

She nodded quickly, and her grimace morphed into a quick, rueful smile.

Wet as she was, Law guessed the resistance to be yet another extension of the tension coiled around and through every part of her.

"Take a deep breath for me."

He watched her rib cage expand and hold at the top of her inhalation.

"Little more," he urged.

She sipped at the air.

"Good. Now let it out. All of it."

Her chest deflated, the velvet walls around him rippling, then releasing.

"Better?" he asked.

"Much," she said.

"Still with me?" He asked this as much to confirm her desire to continue as to gauge whether she might have retreated from her body into the relentless engine of her mind.

Her hand floated upward and pushed a damp lock away from his forehead. "I am."

Only then did Law begin to move again, noting the way her eyes widened and her mouth dropped open in an O of surprise when his cock met on the inside where his palm gently pressed from the outside.

He stilled, drawing his hips back incrementally before pushing them forward to repeat the sensation.

This time, she drew in a surprised gasp.

"Feel okay?" Sweat trickled along Law's spine, his every muscle taut from the effort of restraint.

She tightened her leg around his and seared him with eyes like a blue flame. "More."

All the provocation he needed.

He slid completely out, only to sink in again, angling himself deeper, filling her harder. With every stroke, the knot clenching low and deep between his navel and spine pulsed, sending ripples through his entire body.

If he'd had any doubts about her ability to take all he had to give, they were quickly erased by the ecstatic, almost musical note of rapture she sang into his onslaught. Law wanted to hear that sound again, and always, and then some.

Marlowe anchored her ankles behind his lower back, gripping a fistful of his hair. The wisp of pain amplified the pleasure rising like a wave within him.

He responded in kind, winding his fingers into the short, silky hair at her nape and guiding her upright until their faces were mere inches apart.

They clung to each other, each spurring the other toward the conclusion of the battle they'd begun when they'd first locked eyes. He felt her tighten around him as she scored his back with her nails and bit his shoulder. Sensation ripped along every nerve ending in his body, sending him careening over the edge and into oblivion.

Law roared as he spilled into her with hot, sharp pulses so powerful, they threatened to turn him inside out. He collapsed over her, their torsos glued together by sweat and hearts beating in careless concord as the wind battered the walls.

When he had at last recovered control of his limbs, he pushed himself up enough to see her face, afraid of what he might find there.

Regret.

Disgust.

Disappointment.

Or worse, sadness.

What he saw instead surprised as much as it delighted him.

Amusement.

"Seems this didn't end up being much help in terms of your glassware." She glanced lazily toward the edge of the table. One glass and the bottle of whiskey remained, but barely. The other had fallen to the cement floor, icy shards among an evaporating pool of amber.

"I forgive you." Slowly rising, Law located his work pants and stepped into them.

"I don't remember asking." Marlowe tugged her skirt down and scooted toward the edge of the table, her eyes on the bra and blouse among the tangle of their discarded clothes.

"Stay." He put a hand on her chest to arrest her momentum. "I need to sweep up the shards."

She raised an eyebrow at him. "First, my name isn't Layla, and second, you've failed to notice that you aren't wearing shoes either."

"Maybe so," he allowed. "But I'd also wager I've spent a fair amount more time barefoot than you have." He bent to retrieve the clothing as well as her shoes and returned them to her in a bundle.

"Fair assessment." With practiced movements, she slipped into and fastened her bra and blouse. "Fair Weather Hall was built where an old dairy farm had been, and my mother was constantly warning us about getting tetanus from rusty nails."

Law stuffed his feet into his work boots and shuffled over to a corner where he found the broom and dustpan. "It's no joke."

"You've had it?" she asked.

"No, but two of my brothers did."

Her feet safely shod, Marlowe slid off the table. "Exactly how many of you are there?"

The question needled him more than he expected.

Too many and not enough.

"Four." Using the broom bristles as a buffer, Law scraped the glass into the dustpan.

"Remy is the oldest?"

From Law's crouched position, he watched her slim, shapely calves stroll around the table. Looking at the way the shiny black patent leather hugged her gracefully arched foot, he felt a distinct pang of regret that he hadn't insisted she leave them on earlier. "For all practical purposes."

The shoes stopped next to him, oddly pristine in contrast with the mess of glass and spilled alcohol. "Meaning?"

"Bastien repurposed a shipping container and is living off-grid somewhere in the wilds of Maine. Augustin, we haven't seen since last summer."

Marlowe squatted beside him and took over holding the dustpan so he could sweep without balancing the broom handle on one arm. "He's missing?"

"More like he doesn't want to be found." Law pushed the last of the shards into the tray and stood.

"How do you know?" she asked, resting a hand on the table to help her rise.

Law had to admit that he'd hoped if he danced around the topic long enough, she'd lose interest and change the subject. He should have known better.

His whole life had been spent in this exercise. Deciding how much to tell and to whom. What it might cost him.

"Because he's probably afraid of what I'd do to him if I found him."

"Why?" she asked. "What did he do?"

Suddenly weary beyond reckoning, Law dumped the broken glass into the trash bin and returned to the table. There, he uncorked the bottle and took a swallow. "A lot of things."

"Any chance you could be a little more specific?" Always, the light, teasing tone in which she spoke made compliance seem the only reasonable option.

Law exhaled a long, slow breath. "Stole from the distillery, for one."

Her brows drew inward, concern creasing her face. "Are you serious?"

"Took me a long time to catch on. Augustin was a much better liar than I thought. Or I'm just an easy mark.

I still can't decide which is worse." Another swallow burned its way down his throat, loosening his tongue.

It wasn't his habit to sample his own wares so heavily, and especially not on a weeknight, but this was not a conversation he could have stone-cold sober.

"How did you find out?" she asked.

Law's laugh was bitter as the memory took on sharp lines. "When we were in the early phases of getting 4 Thieves off the ground, Augustin handled everything from the sales side. Always was a smooth bastard. Good with people, you know?"

"A skill he learned from your father?" she ventured, pouring whiskey into the surviving glass in what felt like a conciliatory act.

"How'd you guess?" Law asked, surprised at the sudden jump.

"I imagine the ability to read people and respond accordingly would have been an asset in both the investment and distribution sides of your father's business." She sipped at the tawny liquid with a faraway look in her eyes that led Law to believe the Kane and Renaud patriarchs had more in common than he might have originally thought.

"You're right," he said. "Last June, Augustin went to meet with potential customers in DC. Went radio silent for a few days, which wasn't totally out of character, so I didn't think anything of it. Until I got home from work on day four of not hearing from him, and—" his tongue thickened, resisting the simple act of pronouncing the name "—Jessica, my girlfriend, was gone."

"Gone?" Marlowe asked.

"Gone. Empty closets. Empty drawers. I'd torn halfway through the entire house when I noticed the letter on the kitchen counter." Law seated himself on the edge of the table beside her.

If he'd expected the combination of time and whiskey to sand away the sharp edges of that day, he'd been sorely mistaken. He could still remember how his hands had opened involuntarily when he'd walked into their bedroom and found her side of every surface stripped bare. The bottle of Dom Pérignon fell to the floor and exploded, the bouquet of pink peonies showered with curds of foam.

The sad ruin of a romantic gesture come too late.

"What did it say?" Marlowe's question gently tugged him back into the present moment.

"She was sorry. We'd grown apart over the last couple of years. She hadn't meant to fall in love with Augustin. She felt like they had a chance to build a life together."

Marlowe scooted closer, her hip against the outside of his thigh in silent solidarity.

"The ironic thing is, that's what I thought I had been doing. With the distillery. The house. The land." He gestured toward the warehouse around them. "Building a life."

"How long had you two been together?"

"Six years," Law said. "Four of them good."

Marlowe shook her head. "I can't believe she couldn't even tell you to your face."

Shoulders sagging, Law handed the whiskey bottle to Marlowe. "She tried, I think. Used to tell me we needed to talk more. That I was working too hard. But I was so focused on 4 Thieves that I hadn't realized what was going on under my goddamn nose. They had been gone for a full month before the bonus *fuck you* landed squarely in my lap."

"What was that?" She placed her hand lightly in the center of his back. Oddly touched by the timid nature of her attempt to comfort him and the silence she offered while she did, Law continued.

"Apparently, that life they were building required seed money. Augustin had taken out an additional line of credit against the business in a separate account and defaulted on the payments."

"Jesus." Marlowe's chest deflated. "I'm almost afraid to ask how much."

"Fifty thousand dollars." Saying the number out loud produced the ghost of the familiar, sickening dread he'd felt plowing through paperwork late at night, racking his brain as to how they'd come up with the money.

He'd done it—but at the cost of depleting the funds they'd allocated for the next phase of their expansion. They had already engaged contractors, ordered equipment, requested bids from project management consultants, only to turn around and let them know the project had to be put on hold.

All the while, Law had experienced flashbacks to the humiliation of a kid who made it to the grocery store checkout to discover his father hadn't sent him with enough money to cover everything on the list. His face burning as shoppers behind him sighed and muttered under their breath while he tried to decide what to put back.

"What did you do?" she asked.

Law shrugged. "What *could* I do?"

"Call the police?" she suggested. "Hire a lawyer?"

"Augustin was a signatory on the account and one of

the principals of the 4 Thieves LLC. Technically, what he did isn't illegal."

Marlowe stood. "Your brother lies to you, has an affair with your girlfriend, steals money from the business," she said, ticking the offenses off on her fingers, "and you're just going to let that slide?"

Her words sizzled to the center of his mind like a spark down a fuse.

"What's the alternative? Sue my brother? Pay tens of thousands more dollars to a lawyer, and for what? So I can financially break him?"

"Law, he *stole* from you." She reached out to put her hand on his forearm, but he jerked away.

"Just like he'd been taught. Like we'd *all* been taught." He shoved himself up from the table and turned to face the distillery. "I'm not saying I forgive him or that I'm ever going to forget what happened. But I understand why it did. I'll do everything I can to grow 4 Thieves, but not at the cost of adding more suffering to the Renaud balance sheet. There's already enough to last several lifetimes."

Marlowe was beside him then. A subtle, silky warmth at his elbow. "That's why you're interested in partnering with Kane Foods."

The observation was delivered with such heavy resignation that Law glanced over at her, leveled by the pained look in her eyes.

"Yes," he said.

Her expression softened. "I see."

Law walked to the table and shot the remaining contents of her abandoned glass before raising it in a mock toast. "*Et voilà.* Now you know the distillery's whole sordid history and have everything you need to help your father figure out his next move. Do with that what you will." After recorking the whiskey, he picked up the bottle and turned to her. "Shall we?"

"Shall we what?"

"Rain's let up." He snapped the light off, dropping the axe-throwing area into the after-hours half-light already shared by the warehouse and restaurant. They made their way to the exit, where Law engaged the night security settings on a panel. When it had made the requisite beep, he held the heavy door open for her. "We should be able to make it to the main house without too much trouble."

"Is that anywhere near the staff cottages?" she asked, tucking her blouse into the waistband of her rumpled skirt as she stepped outside. "Remy arranged one of the bungalows for me."

In the rain's wake, the night air held the first hint of the coming fall. Damp, cool, faintly scented of earth and the first casualties of the canopy of summer leaves. In the distance, beyond the silhouette of trees, lightning made a lantern of the low-hanging clouds.

"It's not too far," Law said. His boots crunched on the wet gravel and he walked toward the makeshift carport off the side of the building. "If that's what you'd prefer."

"And what would you prefer?" she asked, confronting her former ATV nemesis with little enthusiasm.

It wasn't something he was often asked, but his answer came readily enough.

"You," he said. "In my bed."

She hesitated for only a beat before swinging into the passenger seat and piercing him with the look of impatient anticipation that was becoming familiar to him. "*Allons-y*, Laurent Renaud."

That familiar phrase coupled with his name in her

haughty purr had him lunging for the driver's seat like he'd been stuck with a cattle prod.

The storm outside might be dying, but the tempest within him had only begun to howl.

Seven

What the hell have I done?

Marlowe awoke with a pounding in her head and an unfamiliar heaviness in her limbs. The pounding was entirely her own fault: just deserts for downing straight whiskey like an eager sorority pledge.

The heaviness? A cooperative endeavor.

Due in part to how deeply she'd slept, and in remainder to the man she'd slept with.

With wasn't exactly the right word. It implied casual accompaniment.

Their arrangement had more in common with tree-climbing vines.

Pressure at the top of her scalp where it was tucked beneath Law's chin. Her arms banded to her naked breasts by his forearm, his fingers like roots around her hand. His long leg thrown over both of hers, the sole of his large, warm foot pressed against her toes. The entire length of her spine flattened against his stomach and chest.

And—a relatively recent development—a growing hardness indenting the curve of her ass.

If she couldn't find a way to extricate herself soon, they'd likely be going for another round.

Their fourth?

Seventeenth?

Somewhere in the strange watches between dusk and dawn, she'd lost count.

Marlowe Kane had no clue how many times she'd had sex with the man whose distillery she'd been sent to audit.

The thought sent a sharpening jolt of guilt and panic careening through her veins.

Eyes still filmy with sleep, she scanned the room for any device capable of relating the time. Though her cell phone was nowhere to be found, her gaze landed on a combination clock radio of the kind that had evaporated from existence save for low-range hotel chains.

At first, she didn't believe the boxy blue numbers.

10:10 a.m.

She fought the urge to sit bolt upright.

On a Tuesday, the recurring Company Roadmap meeting with the executive team would be well under-way.

Picturing her father at the head of the oversize board-room table from which she was conspicuously absent proved the galvanizing thought she needed. She had to get to the distillery office, sift through the last few files she needed and get the hell out of here.

While the sun warmed their braided limbs and tangled sheets, Marlowe slowly began to extricate herself.

Hands, then arms, then legs, in a series of subtle maneuvers that barely seemed to disturb his deep, regular breaths. When she was finally able to curl her pelvis away from the one part of him that was fully, painfully awake and scoot to the edge of the bed, she heaved a quiet sigh of relief.

The respite was short-lived.

No sooner had she put her full weight onto her feet than her body lit up like an accusatory map, reminding her of all the things she'd done…and allowed to be done to her. The sweet, exhausted ache of her inner thighs. The delicious soreness where they met. Nipples so sensitive even the morning breeze from his open window was enough to make her shiver.

Tiptoeing away from the bed, she scanned the room and set about playing a sartorial version of hide-and-seek, donning each garment she found. Her panties hung from the corner of the sleigh bed's mahogany headboard. Her skirt draped over the simple padded bench at its base. Her blouse, which had intrepidly made its way to the oversize leather chair in the corner. Only when she lifted it did she notice the stack of books haphazardly piled on the small table at its side. With an idle finger, she traced their spines to peruse the titles.

Man Enough—Deconstructing Toxic Masculinity. Cry Like a Man—Fighting for Freedom from Emotional Incarceration. The Evolved Masculine and, finally, *The Body Keeps Score: Brain, Mind, and Body in the Healing of Trauma.*

Mouth fully ajar, she turned her attention to a very

large man sprawled across the bed, his erection rising beneath the sheet swathing his hips.

An involuntary surge of moisture dampened her much-abused panties, underpinning a fact she understood with perfect clarity. If she didn't get the hell out of here in the immediate future, her libido would hot-wire her brain and would ride Law into next week.

Regretfully, she allowed herself one last, long look at him before she padded carefully out of his room and toward the stairs. The wood planks proved thankfully quiet, despite their advanced age, as she crept to the living room, where her shoes must surely be.

She was right, it turned out.

One of her heels sat on its side next to the front door.

The other was clamped between the speckled paws of Law's dog, Layla.

They regarded each other with frank suspicion. Layla, lowering her head over her prize. Marlowe, tightening her fists in determination. She briefly considered making a break for it barefoot, but remembering how hard she had rationalized the purchase of these particular shoes—and their conversation about tetanus—she thought better of it.

Steeling her resolve, she moved toward the door with slow, shuffling sideways steps that allowed her to maintain eye contact. Once she'd retrieved the unmolested heel by the door, she tucked it under one arm and held her hands out in front of her, palms open as she took minuscule steps toward the dog.

"Good girl," she whispered. "That's a good girl."

Layla's pink tongue flipped out over her lips as her black nose began to twitch. She cocked her head, round eyes narrowing.

Busted.

Marlowe dipped to pick up a yellow tennis ball, forcing her face to remain neutral when she registered the slimy surface.

"Look what I've got," she said softly, waggling the ball. "Wouldn't you rather have this?"

The dog chuffed, lowered her maw and began to worry the pointed toe of Marlowe's Louboutin with her sharp white teeth.

"No!" she insisted in a gruff whisper as she quietly clapped in the dog's direction. "Bad girl!"

Layla only bathed her prize with a coat of saliva before returning to her efforts.

"That's *it*." Irritation finally trumped the fear, and Marlowe closed the remaining distance to crouch before Law's destructive canine minion. "I know I'm on your turf, but you're going to give me what I want, and I'll clear out of here. I get my shoe, you get your dad, and everyone's happy. Deal?"

"Drop it!" The deep, sleep-gritty voice momentarily disoriented Marlowe enough that she dropped the yellow tennis ball.

Fortunately, Layla was similarly affected. Marlowe snatched her shoe before either one of them had fully recovered their wits. After exchanging a protracted look with her four-legged opponent, Marlowe rose to her feet and slowly turned to face him.

Law stood at the base of the stairs, barefoot, shirtless and wearing only a pair of boxer briefs and a stern expression.

"I don't know which I find more alarming." He yawned, every muscle in his torso waking as he stretched his long arms overhead. "That you thought you could sneak out before I woke or that you were attempting to negotiate with my dog."

"I wasn't *sneaking*," she said. "I just didn't want to wake you."

He raised an eyebrow at her as his arms fell slack by his sides. "Because?"

Hangover dehydration glued Marlowe's tongue to the roof of her mouth. She worked it free with great effort. "*Because* I have work to do this morning before—"

"You can get back to the city?" he finished for her.

She felt gratitude that he had relieved her of the burden of having to be the one to say it. Because they had both known that her departure was inevitable. That last night had been the end.

Not the beginning.

"Yes," she said.

"And you thought if I were awake I'd prevent you from doing that?" He stalked toward her, his feet making no sound on the living-room rug.

Sweat had begun to dampen the armpits of her badly wrinkled shirt. "I just thought it would be easier."

"Easier not to face that you fucked a man you'd only met once? A man whose financial records you'd been auditing at your father's bidding?"

Lava rushed into Marlowe's cheeks. "That is *not* what I was going to say."

He half sat on the arm of a leather reclining chair. "But it's what you meant."

"You don't know me well enough to know what I meant." She stomped over to the couch, grabbed the T-shirt he'd discarded at some point during the festivities of the previous evening and began cleaning her shoe.

Law watched her, arms crossed over his broad chest. "I know that you sound like a teakettle when you're really turned on."

Her nuclear flush deepened.

"That's hardly applicable to the current situation."

"I know that you don't want to be a bridesmaid at your brother's wedding because you think the dress makes you look like a praying mantis."

Marlowe froze as an image of the pale green couture gown flashed in her head.

If he knew about that, what else might she have told him in her passion-hazed state? Her Social Security number? The business identifier code for the Kane family trust? Log-in information for their Swiss bank account?

"Again, entirely beside the point." Setting both shoes on the floor, she stepped into them.

"Mais non, cher." Law rose and walked to her. "I think it's the point exactly."

Sleep had distilled his scent into an intoxicating bouquet of warm, salty skin, a hint of fabric softener from his clean, soft sheets and the musk of an endless night.

A bouquet that convinced her motor cortex that her knees were made of butter.

"How so?" she asked.

He circled her the way she'd seen gallery patrons evaluate a sculpture they intended to purchase. "Way I see it, wearing a dress you can't stand just because the bride asks you to is kind of like coming here at your father's command. In both cases, you're acting against your true nature. You can only do that so long before—" he trailed a finger up the nape of her neck and leaned close enough for his lips to tickle her earlobe "—you *explode*."

And she had.

Again, and again, and again.

"I'm assuming a point is forthcoming in the near future." Despite her icy tone, she felt the heat waking between them—if ever it had slept.

"Stay," he said.

Somewhere beyond the house, a rooster crowed, disastrously late as she would be in a day of her typical life.

"Stay," he repeated. "For a night. For a week. However long you can spare."

"Why would I do that?" she asked.

"Because I want you to."

The directness of his answer made her draw in like a sea anemone. "I can't imagine why. I'm certain there isn't any shortage of women willing to…warm your bed."

"That's just it." His arm snaked around her hip from behind, hand splayed flat over her belly. "A warm bed isn't what I need."

"Then what *do* you need?" She bit her lip, glad he couldn't see her face or the grimace carved into it. Had Neil truly decimated her self-esteem so thoroughly that she now tap-danced for pennies of verbal validation?

"To get you out of my system." His fingers began a quest to her ribs, playing over the ridges with maddening patience.

Marlowe swallowed around a throat full of sand. She'd been expecting something along the lines of "you're here, we screwed, I liked it, let's do it again."

Practicality. Convenience. Both easily understandable, motivating factors.

But this?

This artless admission from a man who had been a monosyllabic ogre not twenty-four hours ago?

"I wasn't aware I was in it," she said.

"You are." He captured her hand and moved it along the length of his rock-hard arousal through the soft fabric of his boxers. "Have been since I saw you sweeping down the stairs like an avenging angel."

She barked a disbelieving laugh. This was not at all how she recalled her entrance.

"Fact is," he said, nuzzling his jaw against hers, "I've been damn near useless ever since, and it's only a matter of time before folks catch on. That's when the real problems start."

Marlowe realized that he had released her hand, and yet she hadn't released his cock. In fact, she had quickened the pace he had introduced. "Problems that affect me in no way whatsoever."

"That's where you're—*unh*—" He groaned as she circled his head with the flat of her palm. "Wrong."

"Highly unlikely." With deft fingers, she found the opening at the front of his boxers and slid her hand inside. "Statistically speaking, I've only ever been wrong approximately 3 percent of the time."

"That math sounds pretty *slippery*." He found the slit in her skirt and bunched the fabric in his fist, but Marlowe clenched her thighs together before he could continue his expedition.

"It's perfectly sound, I assure you," she said.

"I'll just have to pay you a visit so you can explain it to me. Maybe come say hello at the corporate—" Law

sucked a breath through his clenched teeth as she tightened her fist "—office."

"You wouldn't dare."

"You sure of that?"

In fact, she was not. Not even a little.

The image of him filling the doorway to her office shoved her violently back into practicality. Never
mind how the general populace on the twenty-fifth floor
might react to his presence. A state of affairs she found
she could conjure with very little effort.

"One more night?" she asked. "That's it?"

"Mmm-hmm." The vibrating hum of his voice lifted
the fine hairs on the base of her neck.

Now that she had let the idea sink in, Marlowe had
to admit that the prospect of another night in Law's bed
didn't exactly sound unappealing. She could excuse her
absence with a quick phone call. Claim the need for
extra time with the audit because of the storm.

"I'll agree," she said slowly, "on one condition."

"I'm listening," he said.

With how much effort, she'd be hard-pressed to say.

"Tomorrow morning, we part ways, and that's it. No
obscene late-night phone calls, no requests for nudes,
no 'I'm in town for the weekend' or 'what are you up
to' or 'just thinking of you' messages. Once tonight is
over, so are we. Period. Agreed?"

"Depends." He released her and backed away, quickly
rearranging his boxers.

"On?"

"How often you were planning on asking for nudes.
Because as long as it's less than three times a week,
I can probably oblige." Law bent to retrieve the work
pants slung over the couch and pulled them on. Marlowe

fought to keep her eyes anywhere but where the waist-band traversed the lean, sharply cut valley of his hips.

"You know that's not what I meant," she said.

Running a hand through his tousled hair, Law shook his head. "If I hadn't already met your former fiancé, I'd be tempted to ask what the hell kind of men you're dating out there."

"*Former* fiancé and I'm not dating *any* kind of men," she explained. "That's the point."

On a deep inhalation, he lifted his arms in a stretch that made every muscle from his neck to his navel dance in turn.

"First, kind of bold of you to assume I'd even *want* to date you. Second, if I did, that sure as hell isn't the way I would go about it."

Damn him for making her curious how he *would* pursue a woman he wanted for more than just a fling. "We're on the same page, then?" she pressed.

Sunlight spilled through the east-facing window, plating his torso in lambent gold. He closed the distance between them but did not touch her.

"Lady, we're not even in the same book. But if you really need me to spell it out, then, yeah. Once you drive your little blue yuppie wagon off my property tomorrow, I'll happily resign myself to getting the runaround from your dear old dad, and this will be a distant—but pleasant—memory."

Resentment stiffened her spine.

Had she wanted him to disagree with her? Suggest that she was being hasty in her demand?

"Okay," she said. "I'll stay."

"Good." He yawned and shuffled toward the stairs.

"Where are you going?" she asked, less than impressed with the fervor of his reaction to what, for her, had been a significant declaration.

"You're going to need to borrow some clothes, yes?"

Marlowe looked down at her sex-rumpled, grimy blouse and skirt, as dubious about the idea of remaining in them as she was about what he might pick out for her.

"Perhaps," she admitted. "If you have something that would work."

"I might rustle something up," he said, shooting a slightly concerning grin in her direction.

The pattern-seeking engine that she was, Marlowe couldn't help but notice that his words were most spiced with the lyrical, low-country patois he'd tried hard to shed when he was either teasing or turned on.

Both spelled trouble from her current vantage.

Speaking of trouble...she elected to hunt for her phone while she waited for his return. After several false starts, she finally located it in a clumsily shaped and wildly colored ceramic bowl on the entryway table.

Chest tight, she lifted the small device that contained her entire life as gingerly as she might a bomb.

She expected the worst, and she got it.

Barely past ten o'clock, and already forty-plus emails and sixteen missed calls deep. With her nervous system dumping adrenaline into her by the bucketload, she elected to return only one of them.

Luckily, the call's recipient answered on the third ring.

"You do realize the role of black sheep is currently occupied, correct?" Mason said by way of greeting.

Once Kane Foods' chief marketing officer, he had excused himself from the role a couple of months ago when he had fallen ass-over-Aston in love with their father's executive assistant, Charlotte Westbrook. In the days since, he'd directed his boundless energy into the League—once an underground executive fight club and now a nonprofit dedicated to mixed-martial-arts fundraising events. While a new CMO had recently been hired to replace him, Mason still came into the office part-time several days a week to assure a smooth transition.

Tuesdays being one of them.

"I have neither the desire nor skill to unseat you," Marlowe said. "But I do need your help."

"I'm intrigued." The cocky, lighthearted quip shot a dart of unexpected homesickness straight to her heart. Mason had ever been the bright red balloon floating through the storm clouds of her bleak moods.

"I'm out at 4 Thieves distillery for an audit, and I got stuck here last night because of a storm. I might have—" she hesitated, searching for the appropriate words "—overdone it a little. With the sampling."

"You?" The overblown disbelief in his question pecked her with irritation.

"You act like I'm some kind of teetotaling schoolmarm." Unfortunately, as she said this, she caught her reflection in the full-length mirror on the wall behind the front door. The passion-matted hair she'd finger-combed into a bun. The blouse buttoned to her neck. The dour black skirt skimming the tops of her knees.

A schoolmarm—albeit one in need of a working iron—was exactly what she looked like.

"That could be because the last time I saw you cut loose was, let me think…" Mason dramatically drew out the pause. "Never?"

"Maybe that's because you haven't seen me at all since Neil and I broke off the engagement."

A cheap shot, and she knew it. But her hurt frequently drew her lines hastily and in the wrong places. A defense mechanism she both knew and couldn't seem to escape.

"I guess I deserve that," he admitted, his sunny voice dimmed with censure.

"I guess you do." Nothing like doubling down to really set the guilt.

"I know between the wedding and the League, Samuel and I have been pretty self-involved. And probably at a time when you could have used some brotherly support."

Brotherly support.

Just those two words stung a sheen to her eyes that she quickly blinked away. "I'm fine, Mason. Just making the point that a lot has changed lately."

He was uncharacteristically silent for a moment. "I'm sorry, Lo. I should have been there."

His apology balmed her stinging psyche.

"It's okay. I'm sure I was just as oblivious when Neil and I first got together," she said, extending an olive branch.

"No," Mason said. "You weren't."

The implication soaked her, dissolving her attempt at equivocation like so much sugar.

Now the silence was hers. With Mason on the other end of the line, it didn't last.

"Why don't we have dinner tonight?" he suggested. "Just the two of us. If you'll be back by then."

Marlowe hesitated. "The thing is, I kind of…won't. Not until tomorrow afternoon."

She waited for what felt like an eternity for her brother to arrive at the obvious conclusion.

Arrive he did.

"Philomena Marlowe Kane."

She reflexively covered her face at her seldom-mentioned full name, remembering how she had stabbed her arm in the air at Lennox Finch to inform every teacher in every class in every grade ever that she "went by" Marlowe.

"Laurent Renaud?" her brother asked.

"Law," she corrected. "We all had dinner together and then he was teaching me to throw axes, and one thing led to another and…" She trailed off.

"Who are you, and what have you done with my sister?"

"I was going to call Father to let him know that I need another day, but he always does that thing where he waits right until the end of the call to ask you a question that it's almost impossible to answer if you're not telling the truth, and I always break."

"So you want *me* to talk to him," he concluded.

"In short, yes," she said.

"I'm not sure if you remember, but I managed to obliterate my status as favorite pretty thoroughly, right about the time I informed Dad I had zero interest in continuing with the role he'd so subtly shoehorned me into."

Dad.

Mason had been the only one of the Kane siblings to ever casually employ that honorific.

"One, you're still his favorite even if he pretends you're not, and two, you're a far better liar than I am."

"I'm both honored and insulted that you think so," he laughed.

"Please?" Hearing the note of pleading in her voice, Marlowe realized for the first time exactly how much she wanted this. This one day of freedom absent any consequences.

Mason indulged in a theatrical sigh. "Oh, all right. It really is a damn shame how the tornado dropped that cow on your X6. But *so* lucky that you had just enough juice to call me before your cell phone succumbed to its injuries."

"Mason," she warned.

"I'm on it, Lo. Don't worry about a thing."

"You have my eternal thanks," she said.

"While we're on the topic, why stop at just a night? I could buy you at least a week," he offered.

"One night is all I need," she said, infusing her voice with the certainty she needed for herself as well as her brother.

"You're sure?" he asked.

Such insistent sensitivity in her brother's query. Perhaps, with the advent of Charlotte, Mason had, at last, wrested care from the devil.

Marlowe glanced up to find Law descending the stairs with a bundle of clothing cradled in a tanned, muscled arm.

She turned away from the sight, hardening her resolve. "Completely."

Eight

"Where are we going?"

Law glanced at Marlowe, whose gait was somewhat impaired by the rubber overshoes she had selected from the meager options available in the mudroom closet.

He hadn't felt compelled to point out they were the sole survivors of Jessica's exodus. Paired with an over-size flannel shirt and a sundress he had managed to convince her was a gift too large for Emily, Marlowe still made the ensemble look like some New York City fashion designer's idea of a country send-up.

Law repositioned the wide strap of the backpack slung over his shoulder. "You'll see."

She harrumphed. "That phrase got me into a lot of trouble last night, if I recall."

Trouble, yes.

Trouble for them both.

His, the arrow of disappointment fired straight at his chest when he'd woken to find himself alone in the bed. Even more problematic had been the surge of relief when he saw her kneeling on his living-room floor, urgently whispering to Layla.

One night spent together, and already her presence had the power to inflate and deflate him like a balloon. Whether an entire day with her was the best or worst idea he'd ever had remained to be seen.

"Funny," he said, "I don't seem to remember you objecting to a reenactment the second we arrived at the house."

In fact, she'd been the one to initiate the second encounter. He'd barely flipped the dead bolt when she had climbed him like a tree.

"I was already invested by that point," she insisted. "Once you've bought the cow, why not drink the milk?"

"*That* I don't remember you doing. But if it's something you're into…"

She froze at his side, her entire body going rigid. The shift in her demeanor had been so abrupt, so unexpected, that he had continued for several steps without her.

He followed her gaze and saw it anchored on the two horses saddled and tethered to the corral fence.

"Hey," he said, backtracking. "What's wrong?"

"I can't." She shook her head emphatically. "I—I'm not comfortable around horses."

"But you said you played polo."

"*Played,*" she repeated. "Past tense. I haven't been anywhere near a horse since I was seventeen."

"You're just out of practice. Once you're in the saddle, it'll come back to you."

"No," she insisted. "It won't. And don't tell me it's like riding a bike, because bikes don't panic and buck you off."

Fear had shaved a decade from her face, and he briefly saw a frightened girl behind the marble-hard, impenetrable mask she turned toward the world.

Law held still, neither moving toward her nor the horses. "Is that what happened?"

Marlowe hugged her arms to her chest.

"A dog ran into the field and spooked my horse, Gatsby, during the junior-year semifinals, and I got thrown. I broke three ribs and almost got trampled. My father sold Gatsby the next week." She flashed him an angry smile as she blinked away tears. "Happy now?"

Law's jaw ached with the effort of clenching his teeth lest he open his mouth and an unhelpful torrent of abuse aimed at Parker Kane flooded out. He settled instead for "I'm sorry."

Her shoulders lifted in an indifferent shrug.

"Let me tell you about these guys, and if afterward you decide you still want nothing to do with them, I'll let you drive the Varmint instead."

"That thing has a name?" she asked incredulously.

He ignored the barb.

"The one with the white spot on her nose is Rosemary. She was a carriage horse in Philadelphia before she developed arthritis and was surrendered. The big guy is Coriander. He was a draft horse in an Amish community upstate but is enjoying his retirement. I got them both at an auction."

"So, in addition to feeding people who can't afford to pay, you frequent auctions looking for horses to rescue?"

Heat crept up Law's neck. "I wouldn't say *frequent*."

"You are just *determined* to ruin my preconceived notions, aren't you?" Marlowe drew in a deep breath, rolled her shoulders and lifted the crown of her head.

He hovered a pace behind, allowing her space should she decide to retreat.

She gave Rosemary a wide berth, approaching her slowly and from the left at an angle, equine etiquette that must have been subconsciously ingrained in her.

"Good morning," Marlowe said softly, alerting the horse to her location with an audible clue.

Rosemary's chestnut-brown ears rotated backward as she angled her face toward her shoulder, one long-lashed eye taking in the stranger.

Marlowe ventured closer, slowly reaching out a hand.

"She's partial to ear scratches," Law said. Reaching into his pocket, he withdrew several cellophane-wrapped peppermints and held them out to Marlowe. "And the occasional bribe."

Rosemary nudged Marlowe's shoulder with far more gentleness than he'd ever seen her display with Emily.

Amazing, what animals sensed.

"These are terrible for your teeth, you know," Marlowe said in a mock censorious tone as she unwrapped the candy and held it out on a flat palm.

The horse folded her lips over the candy and crunched.

Coriander lifted his head and eyed Law over Rosie's withers, clearly displeased with the treat distribution.

"Will you be okay if I go share with Cory?" he asked.

"Yes," Marlowe said, fingers stroking the silky spot behind the horse's ear. "I think so."

Law ran a hand along Rosie's flank and across her hindquarters as he crossed behind her to divvy out several peppermints to Cory, whose sweet tooth rivaled Emily's in zeal.

Glancing to the side, Law saw that Marlowe now stood directly in front of Rosemary, gently stroking the jagged white line that extended from her forehead to her nostrils.

Then the mare did something that Law had never before seen her do. Lifting her head, Rosemary settled her neck over Marlowe's shoulder, turning her muzzle until the side of her face was pressed against her back.

They stayed like that in silence only interrupted by late-morning birdsong and the hush of wind through the trees. Law found himself so entranced that he was almost startled when Marlowe spoke.

"I want to try," she said.

"You're sure?" Law asked.

She nodded.

Stepping forward to the post, Law untethered Rosemary and draped her reins over the base of the saddle before lengthening the stirrups. "Need any help?"

With an arch of her eyebrow, she wrapped her fingers around the saddle horn, toed one rubber boot into the stirrup and lifted her body with the kind of practiced grace he'd only ever associated with elven warriors in the fantasy novels he'd read as a kid.

"Guess that's a no." He liberated Cory and mounted.

"He's got to be part Clydesdale," Marlowe observed. "What is he? Eighteen hands tall?"

"Seventeen," he corrected, leaning forward to pretend to cover Cory's ear. "But I try not to mention it so it doesn't affect his confidence."

She rolled her eyes and shook her head. "You males and your obsession with measurements."

"Says the woman whose entire life is numbers." Taking the reins in one hand, Law reached down to pat Cory's neck.

"Touché," she allowed. "Do I get to know where we're headed now?"

"How do you feel?" he asked, not answering her question. "Okay with a bit of a walk? We can take it slow."

"Taking it slowly doesn't seem to be our forte." Her lips curved in a mischievous smile. "But lead the way."

Once again, what Law had thought to be one of his better ideas backfired.

From his vantage behind Marlowe in a place where the trail narrowed and they could no longer ride side by side, he watched as her hips rocked in time to Rosemary's gait.

Forward.

Back.

Forward.

Back.

The ghost of a Y-shaped thong panty teasing him beneath the filmy white cotton.

Marlowe turned to him with a question on her face that he'd obviously missed.

"Comment?" he had asked before he could rearrange the verbal wires that surprise often plugged into the declarations of his youth.

She poked him with a knowing smirk. "I asked if you had plans to build anything else on the property."

Hooves beating on the packed earth counted out the space between her question and his answer as he fought a knife-twist of regret.

"We talked about expanding the distillery. Remy has it in his head that we should brew craft beer and mead as well, but I'm hoping it's just the latest in a long line of hyperfixations."

"Like the smokehouse and the dubious vehicles?" she asked.

"Just be glad you weren't here when he was trying to make parchment paper from all the fallen trees. You could smell this place from two counties over."

"Nice of you to be so supportive of all his ideas, though," she said.

The path opened up and Coriander found his way to Rosemary's side.

"Why wouldn't I be?" Law asked. "He was in my corner when the distillery was a distant pipe dream. It's what you do for family."

Clouds passed over her sunny expression. "Not all siblings are so mutually supportive."

Somewhere in the distant trees, the harsh, hectoring call of a crow punctuated her sentiment.

"General observation, or does this apply to the Kane kids directly?" he asked.

She shrugged. "We're as supportive as we know how to be, I guess."

"Meaning your parents weren't so good at it?"

Her jaw was set in a stubborn line. "I didn't say that."

"You do a lot of *not* saying," he mumbled, earning him an arctic glare.

"Because if I wanted to talk about this, I would just hire one of Philadelphia's many top-shelf therapists."

Law turned his torso to face her. "Why haven't you?"

Marlowe heaved an exasperated sigh. "Because I'm *fine*. I'm good at what I do and get paid well to do it. I have a comfortable lifestyle, a social circle of intelligent, successful contemporaries, and access to the best of the fine arts, culture and entertainment. What about any of that suggests that I need the help of a mental health professional?"

He let her question fill the forest, rinsing his mind in the silence before tendering an answer. "The fact that you don't seem to enjoy any of it."

Rosemary came to an abrupt halt as Marlowe tugged the reins.

"What gives you the right to make half-baked assumptions about a life you've been part of for less than a week?"

"So, I'm part of your life now?" he teased. He knew full well he was being a bastard but was enjoying the high color in her cheeks too much to stop.

"You know what I meant."

"I see," he said. "I'm *not* part of your life, but I know you well enough to decipher the intended meaning of your words?"

If she had snatched a branch from the tree and whipped him across the face with it, Law knew it would have been well deserved.

"Just because you have consent to enter my body doesn't mean you have free access to paw at my mind."

Law tugged Cory's left rein to turn him around, walking his horse forward until their bodies were aligned. Her knuckles were white, the edges of her mouth pale.

"Your mind," he said, "isn't separate from your body, by my way of thinking. Anyone who doesn't take care of both isn't worth your time."

"Thanks, *Dr.* Law," she said snidely.

He glanced at her, feeling the same magnetic snap

of connection that had made it impossible for him to look away the first time he'd seen her. Though he knew it was a mistake on every level, he spoke the truth that had clung to him like a burr since that night.

"You deserve better than 'fine,'" he said. "I know I'm not it, but for Christ's sake, stop settling for the least amount of effort and letting those assholes think it's enough."

When she spoke, her voice was even and calm. "Why does it matter to you?"

Something Law had been asking himself even as he delivered his impassioned plea. He gave her the part of the answer he felt safest for both of them.

"Because I have a niece, and if any man were to treat her the way you've been treated, I would crush their necks into pulp with the heel of my boot. I'd prefer not to go to prison for murder, so I'm making damn certain she doesn't put up with that shit instead."

"I'm not your niece," she said softly.

"You're right," he said. "But my niece damn sure wants to be you."

"Point taken." Her posture changed, the vulnerability seeming to evaporate into the rustling trees.

Coriander responded to the directions provided him, turning to the path ahead.

"You still haven't told me where you're going," Marlowe said as their horses fell into step.

"Because we're almost there."

They rode in silence for another ten minutes until Law turned down a smaller path leading deeper into the woods.

The last leg took them up a gently inclined hill. "Keep an eye out for rocks," he advised. "They're both pretty good at picking them out for the most part, but their vision isn't quite as sharp as it used to be."

At the top of the rise, they came to a small clearing where a glass-green pool sat at the foot of a rocky outcropping.

"A spring?" Marlowe asked.

"A hot spring."

Law gripped the saddle and threw his leg over to dismount, registering a subtle soreness in his hips from riding…etcetera. "It was one of the first things that drew us to this property. We only use water from a local aquifer for the distillery."

After anchoring Cory's lead to a tree, he set the backpack at its base and then walked around to Rosemary.

Looking at Marlowe, he offered her his hand.

This time, her hesitation was brief. She dismounted just as gracefully, leaning her weight into his grip as she came down. Their eyes locked for a protracted moment before Law secured the mare by Cory, near enough to an offshoot from the hot springs pool to help themselves to water.

Law unzipped and rooted through the backpack, then handed Marlowe a bag containing cut carrots and apples. She happily took them and walked over to the horses to dole them out.

While she was occupied, he set out the picnic lunch Mira and Grant had packed for him, their brows raised at the request.

A bottle of cabernet, a loaf of French bread, a smoked chicken, a bunch of red grapes, olives, a small, pre-assembled cheese board and a rustic blueberry pie.

"What's all this?" Marlowe asked, returning with the empty bag.

"Lunch," he said. "Hungry?"

"Ravenous, actually."

He knew the feeling. After last night's enthusiastic activities, he had woken to a stomach dissolving its own lining. Hours later, the hastily made toast Marlowe had insisted would be plenty had long since burned off.

"Have a seat," he said.

She settled herself sidesaddle on the blanket, knees and ankles together. "You have plates in that magic bag of yours?"

"Nope." Law began opening containers and setting them out between them.

Her blue eyes widened in alarm. "What do you mean, *nope*?"

"Don't need 'em."

"Am I just supposed to eat off my lap?"

"I could think of worse options." He let his eye take a leisurely journey up her legs until they disappeared into the dress.

"I'm serious," she insisted.

"So am I."

"Well, can you at least hand me a fork?"

"No forks," he said.

"Well, how are we supposed to—" She paused, and Law could see the realization solidifying behind her eyes. "No. Absolutely not. If you think I'm going to use my hands—"

"Of course not," he said. "You're going to use mine."

Nine

Marlowe stared at the spread before her, her stomach gnawed hollow and her mouth watering as the mingled scents wafted up to her. It had the look of a meal you'd find on the unattended table of a witch or a giant in a fairy tale.

Tempting, and totally forbidden.

"You're suggesting that I allow you to feed me…with your bare hands?" She'd thought repeating the proposition aloud would somehow magically transmute it into something resembling reasonable.

It hadn't.

"That's right." Law reclined on one elbow as he popped a grape into his mouth, an almost comical replica of the reclining-satyr sculpture in the gardens at Fair Weather Hall that had made her blush as a girl.

"I'm actually not that hungry." As if in revolt, her traitorous stomach rumbled audibly.

"Liar," he accused.

"How about, I'm not hungry enough to eat from hands that have most recently been on horse tack?" she amended.

With a smirk twisting his lips, Law reached into the backpack, gathered the necessary materials, and proceeded to wash and dry his hands.

Witnessing this, Marlowe told herself it was the food, not the evidence of his forethought, causing the spreading warmth in her middle.

"Now," he said, stripping off his shirt to sprawl beside her. "Close your eyes, and open your mouth."

She gave him a pointed look designed to disguise the small mutiny his words had caused. "If I'm agreeing to eat from your hands, I at least need to be able to see what's in them."

The smooth tawny skin of his rounded bicep brushed her arm as he pushed himself up to an elbow. "What if I tell you?"

"If you're going to tell me anyway, what's the point of my eyes being closed?" Especially when his lightly bronzed, imperceptibly freckled, ludicrously perfect chest was available for visual delectation.

"Marlowe Kane," he drawled, tracing a fingertip over the knobby outcropping of bone at her wrist. "One of these days you're going to run out of questions, and then how will you keep yourself from new experiences?"

"I'm pretty sure eating isn't a new experience," she said. "Seeing as I'm almost thirty and, you know, alive?"

Law reached for the container of riotous red, long-stemmed strawberries, picked one up and lowered it partially into the glass of cabernet. With a garnet drop hanging from the berry, he lifted it to her face. Slowly, he painted her lips with it, letting the wine sink into the seam, then pulling back to brush them with a feather-light touch.

"There's being alive…" His deep voice rumbled near her ear. "And there's *living*. Not the same thing."

Already, her breathing had begun to accelerate.

"Open your mouth."

Marlowe relaxed her jaw, letting her mouth slacken.

"Good. Now close your eyes."

She let them fall closed and was rewarded with the succulent berry stroked across her tongue.

"Bite."

Her teeth sank into the juicy flesh. Whether it was the sensory deprivation or he'd simply acquired the fruit from a superior source that the upscale food store she shopped didn't have access to, Marlowe had never tasted anything so sweet and ripe. Like summer itself, de-voured in one, greedy mouthful.

When she had swallowed, the cool rim of a wine-glass pressed against her lips and she parted them for the slow, steady trickle of wine Law carefully tipped into her mouth. It coated her palate like liquid velvet, heady with dark fruit, oak and spice.

"More?" Law asked.

"Please."

He provided her another sip before she heard a clink, indicating he had set down the glass.

"Bread," he said next, "with creamery butter and some of Grant's blackberry-rhubarb jam."

"Grant as in Grant-from-the-Blackpot Grant?" she asked. The image of that barrel-chested brick wall of a man with wild red hair laboring over canning jars struck her as absurd.

"That's the guy." He brushed her lip with the bread crust, and she obliged.

It was all she could do to keep her eyes from flying open in surprise. "Is that bourbon I taste? And lavender?"

"Affirmative," Law said. "He's our infusions guy. Likes to tinker with different flavors' profiles. Another bite?"

"I mean, I'd hate for something that good to go to waste."

They had progressed through the olives, the chicken and several slices of Honeycrisp apple with sharp cheddar cheese when Marlowe waved her napkin in surrender and opened her eyes.

She blinked at the sudden brightness, amazed at how the leaves seemed a more vibrant green, the sky a deeper blue.

Law, too, had been altered.

His dark eyes glowed a warmer shade of brown, his features having surrendered some of their stony, unyielding edges.

"But you haven't gotten to the pie yet," he insisted, holding up a fat slab. Despite the allure of golden crust and glossy purple-red filling, Marlowe shook her head.

"One more bite and I'm going to pop." She patted her belly, grateful for the loose dress.

"Suit yourself." Lifting the pie to his mouth, Law devoured half the slice in one giant bite.

A different kind of hunger woke as she observed the way his tongue curled to swipe a smear of filling from his lower lip.

"You should at least have some of the chicken before moving on to the pie, don't you think?" she asked, instantly hating the prim, disapproving tone of her question.

His mouth curled in a lazy-cat smile. "You want to feed me some?"

She felt the refusal rise in her throat like an instant reflex but paused before it could escape her tongue.

He hadn't ordered her to feed him. He had asked her if she wanted to.

Did she want to?

Seeing him reclining there, grinning like the biblical serpent from Eden, she was surprised at the answer.

"Breast or leg?" she asked, kneeling over the container.

"Is that a trick question?"

Marlowe rolled her eyes at him. "Breast, it is."

"No objections here." He reached toward her torso, but she quickly swatted him away.

"Same rules apply, sir," she admonished. "Eyes closed, mouth open, hands to yourself."

"I don't remember that last one being part of the deal when it was your turn." Law settled on the blanket. One leg stretched long, the other propped to keep him rolled onto his side.

"You're subconsciously aware of my superior self-control and knew you didn't need to stipulate it." Marlowe peeled off a strip of the tender chicken breast. "Eyes *closed.*"

On a dramatic sigh, Law closed his eyes and opened his mouth.

As he did, the vulnerability of this posture struck her. A man like Law, ever vigilant for potential danger, rendering himself defenseless.

To her.

For her.

A strange privilege, and so sumptuous. To look at a man without being looked at in return. To spend as long as she liked noticing the way his obscenely long lashes feathered the lightly creased skin beneath his eyes. The way his bottom lip was fuller than his top, which crested in sharply chiseled peaks. Or how his left eyebrow—

"I leave this open any longer and flies are going to get in."

Snapping out of her appreciative reverie, Marlowe placed the morsel in his mouth.

Next, she offered him a sip of wine, followed by a slice of the bread, thickly buttered and slathered with jam.

"Just a minute," she said. "I'm going to need the aid of a napkin before the next round."

His hand flashed out and caught her by the wrist with frightening accuracy despite his lack of vision.

"Hey—" she began to protest, "how did you—" But then he brought her hand to his mouth and kissed each fingertip.

"You grip your pens too hard," he murmured.

"How would you know that?"

Having made his way to her pinkie, he jumped back to the index finger and traced the indentation in her fingerprint with the tip of his tongue.

"That," he said. "You'll deaden the nerve if you're not careful."

Her heart had begun to pound in her ears. "And then my axe-throwing days will be over?"

"Among other things." Law moved her finger until it pressed the pronounced indentation between his lips and nose. Had he felt her looking at that precise spot?

"What other things?"

Folding her fingers over, he stroked his tongue along the crease where her index and middle fingers met, flicking the thin web of skin where they joined at the base. When she realized what he was mimicking, Marlowe's cheeks flamed. Inexplicably, the sensation traveled south, waking a sympathetic tingle between her thighs.

He then slipped both fingers between his lips, gently sucking them while Marlowe tried to remember how breathing worked.

Where the hell had he learned to do these things?

Law pulled his mouth away with a wet pop. "Anything else you'd like me to eat?" he asked, his eyes still closed.

"No," she said. "But there's something *I'd* like to."

Encouraged by her boldness, Law sank onto the blanket, hands pillowed behind his head. His heart began to pulse blood south to thicken his cock.

Her fingertips trailed across the bare skin above his waistband. He heard a metallic clink as she undid his belt buckle followed by the *zip* of his fly. Her hands urged him to lift his hips as she shimmied the elastic band of his boxers down to free him.

Feeling the warm breeze across his heated flesh, he cracked an eyelid to find her kneeling to one side of him, her flannel shirt discarded and the sundress climbing up long, pale thighs, a bottle of honey held in one hand.

"Hey," she scolded. "No peeking."

"What are you doing with that?" he asked, head lifted from his sandwiched palms.

"You'll see." An enigmatic smile lifted one corner of her lips. "Figuratively, I mean."

Sighing, he resumed his former position. "You are aware we have black bears in Virginia, right?"

His answer came in the form of a tickling drizzle that began on the right side of his chest, traveled along his sternum and stomach and feathered lower still.

"Then I guess I'll just have to eat you before they do," she purred.

Sensing her movement in a shift of breeze and shadow, he hissed in a breath when her warm, wet tongue lapped at the trail she'd created, painting a lazy circle around the flat of his nipple. Licking. Sucking. Playfully nipping the taut bud at its center. The pain intensified his arousal, flashing like live wire all the way to his root as her mouth moved over his sternum down the ridge separating his abdominals, playing within the grooves.

Her hair tickled the head of his cock, followed the heat of her lips, hovering as she gently blew on the throbbing, sensitized skin.

Restless, electric with the need for control, he burrowed a hand into her silky hair.

"Uh-uh," she clucked. "No hands, remember?"

"That was your rule," he ground out.

"And who do you think is in charge right now?" Her grip tightened around him in demonstration.

Law released her hair, finding fistfuls of the blanket instead. "Are you trying to drive me crazy?"

"Pretty short trip, I hear."

And it was. As soon as her mouth closed over him

and began to move, he had already arrived and was quickly building a base camp.

Crazy. *Crazed.* Mad with the need to touch her. To *feel* her.

Unable to resist any longer, he trailed a hand up the back of her lean runner's thigh as she knelt over him. He shifted her thong to the side.

Parting her silky flesh, he found her already wet. Slick.

Marlowe made a half-hearted sound of admonishment, which he took to be a reminder.

"You didn't say anything about fingers," he said, coating them with her desire.

Her groan vibrated through his skin, linking them in a closed circuit. Her pleasure becoming his, his becoming hers again. Both of them pulled deeper and deeper into the current until he could feel her tightening in random, erratic pulses. Warnings of the oncoming storm.

"Open your eyes," she whispered. Lips glistening with sticky sweetness, she peeked at him through the curtain of her hair. "I want to come with you inside me."

He pushed the strands behind her ear to see her whole face. "Then take what you want."

He'd meant it as an invitation. Daring this siren to sing him straight into the rocks.

A chickadee called out from the trees as the wind rustled late-summer leaves. Marlowe sat on her heels, listening. Beneath her sundress, Law had slowed but not stopped his ministrations.

"It's so...quiet," she breathed in time with the strokes of his thumb.

"All the better to hear you scream."

Teeth sunk into her lower lip, she tugged the ties securing the dress over her sun-dappled shoulders and let it fall to reveal her naked breasts, the rosy nipples already taut in the open air.

Fire danced in Law's blood as she gathered the hem of her dress high enough for him to see his own hand at work in broad daylight, sliding among her swollen, slick folds.

Before straddling his hips, she wiggled out of her thong.

"You all right?" he asked, halting so as not to distract her. "Because you don't have to do this."

Her jaw set in that bloody-minded determination he found so damnably endearing. She yanked the dress over her head and tossed it to the side. "I want to."

Law fought to keep perfectly still despite the bone-deep ache to put his hands on her. His mouth. He needed this to be her decision. Her victory. Severing every invisible leash that had tethered her to anything other than powerful, perfect, savage self.

"That's it, sugar." He placed gentle hands on her hips to let her descend at her own pace without having to rely on the strength of her shaking thighs.

Fingers splayed against his sweat-kissed abdominals, she sighed a long, measured exhalation and sank down until he nudged a place that dragged a guttural moan from her mouth.

Law stroked his thumb over her lower lip, then over her tongue, before returning it to her sex. They moved together.

Her, curling her hips to drive him deeper.

Him, surging upward to meet her until she clenched around him like a vise, tumbling over the cliff and taking him with her.

Ten

Pleasure drunk and completely slack, Marlowe and Law were lying side by side, staring at the sky, when a rustling caught their attention.

They looked over simultaneously and saw Rosemary and Coriander staring at them like they were insane.

Imagining what they must look like, covered in smears of jam and pie filling, breadcrumbs and pastry flakes sprinkled over their hair, Marlowe burst out laughing.

A low, deep belly laugh that racked her abdominal muscles.

Never before had she considered that the term *hysterical laughter* might be more than hyperbole, but every time she looked at the horses, a new gale swept through her, and she couldn't stop. Not when it squeezed tears from the corners of her eyes. Not when her breath came only in rattled wheezes.

Not when the wheezes turned into sobs and shook her body so hard that she felt like her soul might come unmoored.

"Hey," Law said, witnessing the sudden shift. "What's wrong?"

She had no words to offer him. No explanation for what amounted to a humiliating psychological break in front of someone barely more than a stranger.

Marlowe only wept, hunched in a fetal position, pausing only as long as it took to gasp in watery breaths to fuel her silent, body-shaking sobs.

He asked no further questions.

He made no attempt to silence her.

Only gathered Marlowe to his body and held her. Her face buried against his chest, her torso secured in the band of his arms, her knees pressed against his hips and shins against his thighs.

By gradual degrees, the storm passed.

Curled against him, the sobs died to watery sniffles, then to shaky inhalations.

"I'm sorry," she said. "I don't usually do this kind of thing."

"Don't apologize." His deep voice further soothed her raw and ragged nerves.

"I don't know what came over me," she said bleakly.

"A lot of things, probably." Law's hand rested between her shoulder blades, and though Marlowe knew it was impossible, she swore she could feel the warmth of it all the way to her heart.

That, perhaps, had been the chief problem.

A meltdown.

All the pain, the disappointment, the loneliness, the rage she'd kept frozen so long suddenly thawing, only to flood upward and out her eyes.

If this was healing, she wanted to take a hard pass.

Clearing her throat, she stretched her legs long and held her discarded sundress against herself as she sat up. "Well," she said, "that was thoroughly embarrassing."

Law sat up as well, eyes assessing her face as he picked a buttery flake of pastry out of her hair. "Crying?"

"Crying in front of witnesses while stark naked."

Law made a show of looking around. "You're in luck. Rosie and Cory aren't big talkers and I've witnessed much worse."

"Worse than *that*?" she asked incredulously.

"Much," he said.

She dabbed at her stinging eyes with one of the cloth napkins. "I seriously doubt that."

"Well, you've never tried to run me over with a car, for one. In terms of emotional outbursts, I'd say that's worse." Law shot her a sideways grin as he pulled his pants up and got to his feet.

Marlowe resisted the urge to ask for details. "And you were mocking the kind of people *I* date?"

"No," he said, crouching to dip a hand into the pool, "just the kind of men." With a decisive nod, he began to unlace his boots.

"I thought you were supposed to wait an hour after you eat to swim," Marlowe pointed out.

Law lifted a mischievous brow. "I won't tell if you don't."

"How deep is it?" With the lunch she had eaten and the activity that had followed, she felt like she might just sink like a stone.

"Not so deep I can't touch bottom." He peeled off his socks.

"But deep enough that I can't?" She scooted to the edge of the blanket to peer at the water's surface.

"Probably," he said. "But there's plenty for you to hang on to." Shucking both his pants and boxers in one sweep, Law stepped out of them and kicked the garments aside before returning to the blanket. There, he helped himself to a sip of wine and popped several olives in his mouth.

Marlowe didn't consider herself a prude, but she couldn't quite get past just how…naked he was.

"You coming in?" he asked, angling his chin toward the water.

"This spring doesn't run into the distillery, does it?" She had taken the quickest of showers this morning to rinse away what felt like a week's worth of salty sweat but had to admit the idea of submerging herself in warm water from neck to toes sounded like a little piece of heaven.

"Of course not." He grinned at her and stood, sauntering over to the pool and crouching before slipping in legs-first. "That's an infusion I don't think anyone would care for." His dark head disappeared from sight before bobbing to the surface, wet and sleek. He pushed forward and rolled onto his back as gracefully as an otter.

Arms hugged across her breasts, she cast a hasty glance around, rose from the blanket and scampered over to the spring. After testing it with a toe and finding it just hotter than bathwater, she sat and slid in.

Heat enveloped her, loosening her sore muscles and playing about the base of her neck. As her body began to melt, she anchored her fingers on the edge of the rock and extended her legs, pointing her toes to see if they grazed solid ground.

"Careful," warned Law, gliding toward her. "*Parlangua* might get you."

"Par-what?"

"Parlangua," he repeated. "Your basic bayou cryptid. Half man, half gator. All bite. Likes to sample pretty women who go skinny-dippin'."

She yelped as he lightly pinched her bottom beneath the water's surface. "Or so Zap used to tell us," he finished.

"I guess I was lucky." Feet pressed against the rocky rim, she pushed away from the side, executing a lazy crawl that would make her father cringe. "My brothers only ever told me that I was so skinny I'd get sucked down the drain if I got too close to the center of the pool. Well, Mason, anyway. The first time I relayed the information to Samuel, he explained that it was scientifically impossible."

Marlowe arched her neck to let the warm water work on her scalp, still not quite ready to completely submerge her face. When she brought her chin to her chest, she found Law smiling.

"What?" she asked.

"Just never seen you look so…wild." His hand rose from the water to tuck a dripping tendril behind her ear. The pad of his finger traced the cartilage, following it to the lobe and continuing to the curve of her jaw to her chin, where he pressed his fingertip to the barely visible cleft. All the while tracking the journey with his eyes.

"Please," she scoffed. "This is the wildest thing I've ever done in my life."

He cocked his head and grinned at her. "The day is young."

Eleven

Marlowe lay on the blanket, content, drowsy and bone-less. After their soak, they had cleared the food and sprawled out, letting the breeze dry them. Which then led to them falling asleep together and waking just as the setting sun began transforming the sky into a tie-dyed veil of vermilion and gold.

"Think they've sent out a search party yet?" she mumbled sleepily.

Law's fingers trailed up her spine. "Not until tomorrow morning, at least. I put them on notice that any biped spotted within a mile of this place would be subject to my wrath."

She peeled the side of her face from his chest. Her ear ached from where it had been compressed between his pectoral muscle and her skull. "You *told* them?"

"I told them this area was off-limits. Not that you were going to drizzle honey on my—"

"Not another word, Renaud," she said, picking through the pile of their discarded clothing and sorting out the items. When they were both dressed, she set to rolling up the blanket while Law resaddled the horses.

"I suppose we ought to get heading home," he said. "Wouldn't want these two to miss feeding time."

"I wouldn't much mind feeding time myself," Marlowe replied.

Law smirked at her over Coriander's back as he adjusted the stirrups. "Someone's appetite sure has improved since her arrival yesterday morning."

Had it only been yesterday?

Marlowe felt like she'd been here for at least a week. Maybe a month. Perhaps in part because she'd had more sex in the last twenty-four hours than she had in the last quarter of the fiscal year with Neil.

In the tall grasses bordering the clearing, a chorus of crickets took up their evening song as they both mounted and began the ride back to the distillery. She drew in a deep breath, filling her lungs with the scent of the woods, wishing she could keep it within her. Wishing that she could wrap this peace around her and carry it home.

"What's going on in that head, *cher*?"

"Hmm?" She looked over at Law and realized several moments had passed since he'd spoken.

"Where'd you go?" he asked.

"What do you mean?" The question didn't sound as light as she'd meant it to. "I'm right here."

"No." He shook his head. "You're a thousand miles away already."

Already.

The word hung over this beautiful sunset like the blade of a guillotine. An inevitable end, quickly approaching. She had expected to feel relief at the prospect of returning to her life after having been so roughly evicted from it over the course of this day. Hell, she wasn't even wearing her own underwear.

And yet...

And yet.

"Look," Law said.

Marlowe lifted her eyes to a sight that made her gasp.

Fireflies. Hundreds of them. Maybe thousands. Floating like fairy lanterns among the trees.

Neither of them spoke as the horses walked into the twinkling blizzard. Tiny lights danced around them, winking out only to appear elsewhere. Above them and around them and behind them. Her heart grew so light, she felt in danger of it lifting her like a helium balloon.

"Isn't it amazing?" she whispered.

She turned to Law when he didn't answer and instinctively knew that he hadn't been watching the fireflies. He'd been watching *her* watch them.

"Yes," he agreed after a beat of silence. "It is."

Marlowe woke early the next morning in a cocoon of cold sweat. There in the blue-gray darkness of predawn, her mind ticked like a clock. *My father. Law. 4 Thieves. Kane Foods. My father. Law. 4 Thieves. Kane Foods.* She gave up on trying to coax her brain to switch off after about an hour and slipped out of bed. Adding a pair of Law's sweatpants to her already-stunning sleep ensemble of underwear and one of his T-shirts, she dashed off a quick note in the event that he woke while she was gone.

Downstairs, Marlowe borrowed boots and a jacket from the hall closet and let herself out the front door. She was so pleased that she had closed it without a single squeak that she had to stifle a scream when she turned and saw a man sitting on the porch swing.

"Remy." She pressed her hand against her chest to quiet the wildly beating heart beneath. "What are you doing out here so early?"

He leaned forward, propping his elbows on his knees. "Hoping I might run into you, actually."

The first fingers of alarm worked at her gut. Remy had been noticeably subdued at the dinner last night despite the Blackpot operating at full tilt. Cheerful patrons and Johnny Cash on the jukebox. Emily chattering away like a little bird.

Truth was, Marlowe didn't know him well enough to think anything of it.

"What was it you thought I would be doing on the porch at six o' clock in the morning?" she asked, arms folded across her chest.

Eyes as gray as the iron dawn lifted to her face. "Sneaking out."

"I hate to disappoint you," she said, electing to adopt a lighthearted tone despite the accusation, "but I was just going for a walk."

"All right," he said, rising. "Let's walk."

Their boots made a hushing sound as they tromped through grass wet with dew. Fog hung lacy over hollows, waiting to be burned away by the sun.

"You know, when Law first talked about building a distillery, I thought he was crazy." Remy sidled up to the empty horse corral, gripping the top board with weathered hands.

"It's a pretty ambitious undertaking," Marlowe agreed.

"That's the thing about Law." Remy's cheeks creased in a wistful smile. "Since we were kids, he's been like that. Big dreamer, even then. When things got really bad at home, we would sneak out through my bedroom and climb on the roof. Talk about having land someday. With a pond and trees for a rope swing. Room for a horse or two."

Not for the first time, Marlowe noted Remy's lilting cadence of speech, a more concentrated version of Law's slight accent. The picture it painted pierced her. Two lonely dark-haired boys trying to speak a better life into existence.

"Being a dreamer is a good thing," she said. "Having the tenacity to make it come true is a better one."

"If it's being applied in the right direction. Otherwise—" he shrugged "—you're just pissing up a rope."

A cold heaviness had begun to spread in her chest at this turn in the conversation. "That's a rather colorful visual."

He turned to face her. Though a few inches shorter than his brother, Remy's broad shoulders and powerfully muscled torso made him just as formidable. "I'm going to ask you a question, and I want an honest answer."

She braced herself. "What's that?"

His eyelids lowered a fraction as he assessed her face. "What's your game, lady?"

"I'm not sure what you mean," she said.

"Come on now, *cher*," he said. "It's just us. You can drop the act."

Marlowe blinked at him. "Act?"

"You roll into town, you eat at my table, you play

princess with my little girl, and then you seduce my brother."

Spots danced at the edges of her vision. "Are you serious?"

"One of us ought to be." He leveled her with a glare of such contempt that Marlowe physically winced. "I may not be a suit-wearing-executive type, but even I know that's not what you do when you're sent to audit an investment."

Direct hit.

The gnawing guilt she'd been trying to push away this morning began to cloud her brain. "What happened with Law is none of your business."

"But it *is* my business." He took a step closer, his voice lowered to a deceptively silky register. "I poured everything I've got into 4 Thieves. Every damn penny. Not because I wanted a goddamn yacht or jet. Because I wanted my daughter to be the first Renaud who can go to any college she wants. So she can have a future and choices I didn't."

The earth shifted beneath the rubber soles of her borrowed boots. She felt herself losing ground, standing here in front of Emily's father trying to look like anything other than the irresponsible, undeservingly wealthy opportunist she really was.

"This last year," Remy continued, "I've watched Law lose the woman he loved to Augustin and nearly lose the business he's worked so hard to build because of it." He shook his head in disgust. "I've never in my life seen a man work as hard to come back from something like that."

The early morning quiet stretched between them.

"I'm not trying to interfere with that, Remy," she said. This part, at least, was true.

"Funny how good a person can be at something without actually trying, isn't it?" he flung at her.

"What I don't understand," Marlowe said in a more measured tone, "is if you don't trust me, why not talk to Law directly?"

"Because he's too damn stubborn to listen to me." Remy threw up his hands in frustration. "And when it comes to women, he has a blind spot a mile wide."

Yes, she thought, *he certainly does.*

"I'm not exactly sure what you want from me." Gazing out over the empty corral, she felt a distinct tug toward the stalls attached to it. Longing to stroke Rosemary's warm, velvety muzzle. To feel the comfort of being treated gently by an animal so large and powerful.

Remy propped an arm on the fence to study her in profile. "The truth. For months now, Parker Kane has strung us along, and then he sends you, after we've already been through a due-diligence process. I want to know—I want you to look me in the eye and tell me—that an audit is *all* he sent you to do."

In any other setting, she would have replied with some scathing remark or equally effective deflecting sentiment. But something about this man's simple, earnest observation propelled her straight to the unvarnished truth.

"My father is a—" she paused, searching for the right word, knowing there wasn't one "—proud man. Over the course of this transaction, he hasn't felt that 4 Thieves…sufficiently appreciated the opportunity Kane Foods was offering. So, he thought that I 'might be able to perhaps analyze your financial data in a way that better reflects your level of commitment,' in his words. In mine, he made it clear that this was what was expected of me."

However bitter the words had felt on her tongue, some part of her lightened once they'd been spoken. "I do what's expected of me, Remy."

The corners of his mouth turned down. Only then did she notice the smooth terrain of his previously stubble-flecked jaw.

He had shaved for this conversation. That, somehow, made all of this worse.

"*Cher*, if there's anything I understand, it's the influence a father can have. For the good, or for the bad." This time, the *cher* sounded a good deal more like the one he'd employed when speaking to Emily, and for some goddamn reason, this stung tears to Marlowe's eyes. "I can't tell you what to do when it comes to Parker Kane. But I can tell you what I know about my brother. You tell him what you just told me, and he's not going to look at you like he did at dinner last night."

Chipped paint from the corral crackled beneath her fingers as they tightened on the plank. She couldn't speak. Couldn't think of a single relevant thing to say.

"You got what you need to finish what you started. Guess you have to decide what it is you really want." Remy gave her a hard look and turned to walk toward the main distillery building, leaving her stinging from his acid invective.

Marlowe took her time getting back to the house, thinking as she shuffled along. After toeing her boots off on the porch to avoid dragging in the confetti of cut grass, she quietly opened the front door and crept inside.

Upstairs, she found Law exactly where she'd left him.

Asleep in bed, only a sheet covering him to the waist. One powerful arm dug beneath the pillow, the other outstretched, long fingers splayed, reaching for her unoccupied spot.

Her heart froze into a lump of lead in her chest.

Remy was right.

The confirmation came to her in a thunderclap of clarity.

It wasn't just the sight of Law. It was the scent of his warm skin still clinging to her. Remnants of wood, soap and whiskey. It was this room, and the closet still standing empty, and the impromptu gallery of brightly colored drawings eating up most of the south-facing wall. It was his neatly hung clothing and nearly empty hamper. The stack of books on his side table.

A man who could and did take care of himself.

A man who took care of others.

A man who had taken care of her.

A man who wouldn't want to, if he knew the truth.

Law woke with the last few wisps of a pleasant dream clinging to his mind. He yawned and stretched, his overworked muscles making themselves known in a cascading catalog of complaints.

As his limbs expanded across the mattress, recognition of what they *didn't* encounter caused his sleep-fogged eyes to widen.

No Marlowe.

Two nights, and already his body had instinctively tuned itself to her presence.

And absence.

He told himself it was curiosity, not concern, that had

him sitting up and quickly slipping on a pair of athletic shorts before taking to the stairs.

Just as he told himself it was recognition, not relief, he felt when he found her kneeling before Layla just as she had been the morning before. Only this time, instead of attempting to barter for a shoe, she was mumbling softly and slowly stroking the dog's ears.

"I seem to be having déjà vu," he said softly so as not to startle her.

Her being Marlowe, who seemed much more careful of Layla than the dog was of her.

"You're up." As she began to rise, Law's stomach sank. The tension had returned. Stiff limbs. Rigid posture.

As if the last forty-eight hours had evaporated, and all they had said and done right along with it. She'd even changed into the outfit she'd arrived in, rumpled clothing and all. By the door, her purse and laptop bag sat at the ready.

A truth written all over her face. The pale cheeks, the sunken corners of her lips, eyes that wouldn't quite meet his.

Law descended the stairs, taking care to keep his strides even and calm despite the chain reaction of familiar thoughts lighting up his brain like a Christmas tree.

His own words returned to him like a vicious boomerang.

I know I'm not it, but for Christ's sake...

He had said this to her. Reassuring her that he was capable of handling whatever this would be.

He had lied.

And now here she was. Another woman who couldn't wait to be on the other side of his door.

What did you expect?

This was the kindest of the questions echoing inside his head.

The others shaved much closer to the bone and came to him in a gravelly, booze-wet voice he'd tried to evict from his head.

What possible use could a woman like Marlowe Kane have for a man like you?

Did you honestly think you had a chance?

He hadn't. Not really.

Standing before her, feeling disappointment push down like bricks set on his shoulders, he had no choice but to admit it. Some part of him had begun to hope. For what, he didn't know. Didn't *want* to know, for that matter.

"You're leaving." He let it be the statement it was rather than the question he wanted it to be.

Her head dipped downward in a slow, mechanical nod, her gaze straying to the window pouring golden light across the old wood floor. "Yes."

Law folded his arms across his bare chest, an unintentional but obvious gesture of self-protection. "What happened?"

"Reality, Law." Marlowe swept an arm wide as if mentally demolishing the wall that separated them from the outside world. "Waking up to an inbox just about ready to collapse what remains of my data storage. Dozens of missed calls. All while we were out in the woods yesterday carrying on like a couple of horny teenagers."

Listening to her impassioned words, Law studied her mouth, her eyebrows, all the places he'd learned to watch for her emotional tells. The upset was real. The reasons she attributed it to? *Off.* Hollow. Strange.

"Marlowe," he said, waiting until her eyes came grudgingly to rest near, if not on, his. "You can talk to me. You know that, right?" He reached for her hand, but she yanked it away on a frustrated sigh.

"Talking is the last thing I want to do. Every time we do, you just won't quit. Picking, picking, picking at every place that hurts, waiting for me to unravel. Well, congratulations. Mission accomplished. You witnessed a rare spectacle. But if it's all the same to you, I'd like to get back to my real life, where I can go entire months on end without having my heartstrings played like a Stradivarius."

"It won't." Law ventured a step into the black cloud of her ire. "When you leave, it won't be the same for me."

Their eyes met, and he knew she had taken his meaning.

"Don't do this, Law," she said quietly. "Please."

Law willed his tongue to loosen, but the familiar chorus held it fast.

Don't say it. If you say it and she leaves anyway, you know how stupid you'll feel? Do you really want to go there again?

It was the *again* that decided it.

"You know the one thing that separates truly great whiskey from the mediocre shit?" he asked, not bothering to wait for an answer. "It's not the mash or the first distilling or the second. It's knowing when the head ends and the heart begins. It's knowing when you've reached the part worth keeping. I know, Marlowe. I know that despite everything you're saying right now, there is something between us worth at least trying to keep."

She met his entreaty with an accusing look. "Unlike your promise that you could handle this?"

It was a fair indictment. At the time, he thought he could. "That was before."

"Before what?" she snapped.

"Before I realized that I would rather regret telling you how I felt than regret never knowing what might have happened if I did."

Disappointment moved across her face in slow motion. Crumpling her brow. Glazing her eyes. Flattening her lips. A head-on collision of unwanted information.

"Law." She took a step backward and sank onto the leather couch. "You don't feel nearly as much for me as you think you do."

He remained standing, not entirely trusting his feet to carry him across the room without betraying a nervous twitch. "I think that I might just be a more accurate judge of that, don't you?"

"No." She slowly shook her head. "I don't."

"How do you figure?" he asked.

Marlowe worried a loose thread in the hem of her skirt. "I don't know that this is going to be a productive conversation for us to have."

"I want to know," he insisted.

When she looked up at him, her expression had softened. "Your mom took off when you were just a boy. Your father proved an unreliable parent, at best, and you spent most of your adolescent years attempting to navigate a volatile situation by taking care of the people around you. People who, by all rights, should have been taking care of you. When you were old enough, you worked your way through a string of girlfriends, all of whom took advantage of your caring nature. None of whom lasted very long. Until you get to Jessica.

"Jessica actually stuck by you for several years," she continued. "Which made you think you'd finally found someone who'd support you the way you've always supported everyone else. And then she stabbed you while you were working yourself to death trying to build a future not only for her but your entire family."

Law felt rooted to the spot, invisible cicadas droning in his ears.

"Then you meet me. There's nothing that I need you to give me financially other otherwise, so, if I agree to stay for a few days, it must be because of who you are and not what you can *do*. You like how that feels, and you're confusing that as feelings *for* me."

In all his efforts to understand how the Renaud family had ended up the way they had, Law had arrived at some of those same conclusions. But never had they been distilled to a bitter draft and spooned down his throat.

He felt himself losing his grip on the calmer, more reasonable version he had labored to build over the last year. Pain no longer yielding truth but volcanic anger. Belching ash until it blotted out the last of his reason.

"You're a coward."

Marlowe sat straighter, obviously preparing to defend her point. "Excuse me?"

"You're doing everything you possibly can to convince yourself that the only reason you agreed to stay is to scratch an itch, when the truth is, there's a part of you that's so miserable, you would risk everything to avoid returning to your cramped, claustrophobic life."

Her mouth dropped open as she glared at him with eyes glittering like chips of ice. "You don't know the first thing about my *real* life."

"No?" he challenged. "How about this? You want to blame patterns of parental neglect? Let's talk about your father and how every man you've allowed into your bed is a disappointment. Let's talk about how your entire life, you've done exactly what was expected of you, even when it's killing your soul and stealing any chance you have at happiness."

Her hair swung around her chin as she shook her head. "I don't want to hear any more."

But he couldn't stop. Could no longer bear the pressure building inside him.

"On the night we met, you accused me of stripping you with my eyes. At least *I* could admit I was doing it. I looked and you looked right back. You have *been* looking since the day you arrived here. I've been all too happy to oblige. To give it to you as rough as you want it and hold you just as gently. To let you think you're doing *me* a favor by playing hooky when I was giving you permission to do what you already wanted to do. All of that, I accept. What I don't accept is you tucking your tail and running, and then pretending there's nothing to run *from*. Because what I've felt while you're here scares the shit out of me, but at least I have the guts to say it."

Tiny quicksilver crescents gathered on her lower lids and spilled over her cheeks. The corner of her mouth jerked erratically as she fought to stop her chin from quivering.

Shit.

He had made her cry.

Just another bully in the long, twisted Renaud line.

But something in him wouldn't bend, couldn't bend, despite the instant wash of remorse. He had already bared too much of his soul and he knew she would never do the same.

"I'm going to need a ride to my car," she said flatly, dabbing at her cheeks with a tissue.

Too tired to argue, Law pulled on a T-shirt and jeans upstairs and returned with his keys.

Marlowe had risen from the couch and stood statue-like by the door, her laptop bag slung over her shoulder and her purse and trench coat hanging from the other arm. Her cheeks were dry and her chin lifted, all traces of vulnerability utterly eradicated.

Grudging admiration swelled Law's heart even as the dull ache in his chest deepened. Pride worn like battle armor. The Valkyrie restored.

Their ride to the smokehouse seemed to take twice as long as usual, both of them in fossilized silence.

When they reached her BMW, they found it coated with a film of powdery dust, pebbled with the remnants of dried raindrops.

Marlowe levered herself out of the seat even before they'd pulled to a full stop, as if she couldn't be away from him quickly enough.

"Thank you," she said brusquely, striding toward her car. "Someone will be in touch once I've had the chance to review what I've gathered." She aimed her key fob at the vehicle and it emitted a perfunctory chirp as the locks disengaged.

"Marlowe." Her name was gravel in his throat, raspy and more urgent than he would have liked for her to hear.

Shoulders still set, she glanced back, giving him a

last look at the elegant angles of her profile, her eye set in her silky cheek like an aquamarine, the subtle spray of freckles across her nose already beginning to fade.

"You deserve better than fine."

Then she slid into her car, turned over the engine and drove out of his life.

Twelve

Seething, Law crested the stairs leading to the office loft to find Remy at his desk, a stack of shipping logs in his hand and a look of concern creasing his features. "What is it? What happened?"

Law tossed a sheaf of papers bearing the Kane Foods crest and the cardboard FedEx envelope they'd arrived in on the desk before his brother. "Read for yourself."

Watching his brother's eyes scan the page, Law could pinpoint the precise second when Remy had reached the same line of text that had sent his own blood pressure shooting through the stratosphere.

His brother's entire body tensed as if bracing for a blow. He looked at Law, shock, confusion and dismay warring for supremacy on his hard-bitten face. "Kane Foods is canceling the distribution to 4 Thieves?"

Just hearing it spoken out loud drew a red curtain

of rage across Law's vision. His hands flexed, then straightened, then flexed again, itching to break something. To find a wall to add several new holes to. "Looks like it."

"They keep us dangling like a worm on a hook for months now, drag us through this whole goddamn process just to cut bait and run?" The empty coffee mug on Remy's desk jumped as he slammed the papers down.

Law was less surprised by this turn of events, however much they infuriated him. Cutting bait and running was something the Kanes did very, very well.

Remy wilted in his chair, lines chiseling deeper into the corners of his eyes. His brother aged a decade in that moment.

Had he torn the papers and hurled them over the wood railing or put his boot through a box, it would have been a relief.

But the dead, dull stare his brother turned to the distillery's gleaming copper heart filled Law's gut with hot, sick regret.

"Go ahead." He steeled himself. Ready, eager almost, for the inevitable confrontation.

In the seven weeks that had elapsed since Marlowe Kane's visit, Remy had kept odd hours. Coming in before dawn to take care of paperwork, inventing tasks that required him to be anywhere on the property Law was not.

He suspected he already knew the reason for this and hoped maybe this new development would force them to finally address it.

The desk chair squeaked as Remy pushed himself back, his expression blank. "What?" he asked tonelessly.

Law pulled his shoulders back, driven by the sub-conscious need not to make himself a larger opponent but a larger target. "Go ahead and say it."

His brother reached for the coffee cup, floated it to his lips, registered its emptiness, mechanically set it back again. "Say *what*?"

Grateful to have a task, Law retrieved the coffeepot and refilled the mug, feeling a tug at the tiny avalanche of grounds as he poured out the dregs.

"Say that I'm an idiot for holding out for the Kane Foods offer." Acrid fumes rose from the pot as he shoved it back into the caddy and flipped the Off switch. "That I'm a titanic hypocrite because I warned *you* not to touch Marlowe Kane but I couldn't keep my hands off her, and now we'll have to go back out and find a different investor for the expansion as a result."

A shadow banked in Remy's flint-gray eyes. His jaw ticked beneath its crust of dark stubble. "I can't say that."

Stalking across the loft, Law slung himself on the leather couch. The initial blast of nuclear wrath had boiled away, leaving him spent and brittle. "But you're thinking it."

"I'm thinking that it's a damn good thing this is a distillery, because I need a drink." Using the knife he always had clipped to the pocket of his jeans, Remy slit open one of the boxes of rye and returned to the desk with a bottle. After dribbling a healthy slug into his cof-fee, he held it out to Law in a silent invitation.

Though the clock hadn't yet struck ten, he accepted it and took a swallow in solidarity. Cool glass against his lips. Fiery liquid trickling down his throat. Memories of thunder rumbling from the last time he'd sipped straight from the bottle.

During the storm. With Marlowe Kane.

The roar of the rain on the corrugated tin roof mingled with her carnal cries still haunted his ears.

"You ever miss him?" Remy asked, reeling Law back to the present.

"Who? Augustin?" A guess, as his embezzlement was what had led them to secure an investment in the first place.

Gripping his spiked coffee, Remy downed another swallow. "Zap."

Law glanced at his brother, surprised at the unforeseen detour from their current situation. "Relevance?" he asked.

"I mean, sure, he was a thief and a liar and the reason all us boys ended up in the can by the time we were old enough to drink," Remy quickly added.

All us boys, *except* Law. Not because he hadn't participated in the family hobby of lifting useful items that didn't belong to them, but because, as the youngest, his brothers made sure that Law never got caught.

"Still waiting for the 'but.'" Law took another tug from the bottle.

"*But*," Remy said, "Zap always had a plan."

In all the memories they shared, he couldn't once recall his brother addressing their father as "Dad" or "Pops," as he and the rest of his siblings had. For the first time in his life, it occurred to Law to wonder why.

"I think getting out of our current spot would have been a hair out of his depth."

"Probably," Remy allowed, one corner of his mouth curling into a crooked smile. "Would have been pretty satisfying to see him light up a bag of horse apples and leave them on Parker Kane's doorstep, though."

No way did the man answer his own door, but the mental image of the iron-haired tycoon swearing and stamping his polished loafers into flaming mounds of manure filled Law with a spasm of misanthropic glee all the same. "Can't argue that point."

Draining the last of his coffee, Remy set his mug aside.

Thus fortified, he turned his attention to the stack of papers. "This is all they sent?"

"I didn't check," Law admitted. He'd gotten only as far as "on behalf of Kane Foods International, we regret to inform you" when his world began to tilt on its axis.

Remy felt around the pocket of the express packet and brought out a small pale blue envelope. "What's this?"

Pressing his knife into service once more, his brother worked it under the blob of wax stamped with an elaborate letter *K* sealing the flap, then turned it over to reveal an elegant bramble of cursive on the front. "Got your name on it."

He lobbed it at Law like an angular Frisbee.

Anticipation and dread tangled in his chest as he caught it.

From *her*?

The card he pulled out was of such fine stock, it almost felt buttery between Law's fingers.

An invitation.

To Samuel Kane's wedding reception.

All ambient sounds of the distillery's daily activity dissolved as his head filled with pulsing static. Seeing a small arrow drawn in blue ink on the bottom of one corner, he turned it over. He stared at the handwritten words so hard, they were embossed on the backs of his eyelids when he blinked. "The hell?"

"What is it?" Remy asked.

Law flicked it onto his desk. "See for yourself."

"Why would Samuel Kane send you an invitation to his wedding?" Remy's eyes lifted to Law, who had begun to pace the length of the balcony, hands balled into fists at his sides.

"Reception." He turned on his boot heel and pinned Remy with an irritated glare. "Read the back."

Remy squinted at the text, a few more creases spreading at the sides of his eyes than Law remembered. "'Please come. We need to talk. MK,'" he read aloud. "What the hell does that mean?"

Damned if Law knew what they could possibly have to say to each other at this point. He'd rehashed their final conversation a thousand times. Sometimes changing his part of it. Sometimes hers.

But it always ended the same.

With him sorry, and her gone.

"It means Marlowe Kane wants me to come to her brother's wedding reception."

"Brother." Remy let the card fall to his cluttered desk and slowly shook his head. "If this doesn't show you what she was about all along, I don't think anything can."

Fighting an irrational surge of defensiveness despite the circumstances, Law made himself draw in a steadying breath. "I'm not sure I want to know what you're getting at."

"For nearly two months, you've been moping around here like a lovesick teenager without one goddamn word from her. Then she thinks she can just *summon* you and you'll come running like some pathetic lapdog? She couldn't call you? Text you? Use pretty much any means other than an invitation to her brother's wedding in the same damn package as the letter telling us that Kane Foods is canceling their investment?" Anger darkened Remy's irises to a steely gunmetal gray in the shadowed sockets beneath his lowered brows.

"We don't know that she—"

"Wake the fuck up, *Laurent*." Remy slapped a palm on the desk with a resounding crack. "Her father is *Parker Kane*. If you don't realize that Marlowe did exactly what he sent her here to do, you're an even bigger fool than I thought."

Fool.

Better to be called almost anything else. Bastard. Jackass.

But a fool? *This* had been the deadliest insult in Zap Renaud's book. A verbal dunce cap advertising your ability to be taken advantage of. Humiliated. Used.

That his brother had hurled it so casually meant it wasn't the first time it had crossed his mind.

"What *exactly* did she do?" Law knew this was a dangerous question to ask, an invitation to skate onto the rapidly thinning ice between them.

"You really need me to spell it out for you?" A warning flashed bright and sharp in his brother's eyes, his head lowered like a ram's.

But their horns were already locked.

"I do."

Remy stalked over to the railing. His work-chapped hands gripped wood they had salvaged in those hopeful early days.

"You pissed Parker Kane off. Failed to properly fawn over the honor of being considered by Kane Foods. So he sent Marlowe to find something that would allow him to undercut his original bid for 4 Thieves. Teach us a little humility." Remy stiffened. "Looks like he decided we needed a different lesson."

Cold fingers walked over Law's skin. "How do you know that?"

More of the distillery floor became visible as his brother's shoulders rounded. "She told me. The morning she left."

"You…talked to her the morning she left?" Law asked, pieces slowly clicking into place.

Shortly after Marlowe's BMW had disappeared down the dirt road in a chalky cloud, he had returned to the house and gone straight to the bedroom, intending to strip the bed. To rid it of the scent of honeysuckle, rain and silk. The scent of *her*. As he'd grabbed her pillow, a note had fluttered to his feet.

Going to stretch my legs. Be back for breakfast.
—M
PS: You're breakfast.

He'd stood there, stunned dumb, wondering what had changed between the time she'd written it and returned from the walk with a face full of storm clouds.

Now he knew.

Law dropped his shoulders down from his ears and willed the tightness in his chest to release. Only when he'd cycled through three whole breaths did he allow himself to speak.

"What did you say to her?" he asked.

Because he had absolutely no doubt his brother had said *something*.

Remy met the question with stony defiance. "I told her the truth. That I was willing to put up with Parker Kane's puppet shoving her nose in our records but not her hands down my brother's pants."

Law felt a wave of déjà vu so acute it made him dizzy.

Fistfights had been a rite of passage for the Renaud boys. You test your strength against each other first. Because the world will be worse.

Law and Remy had fought only once.

Then, too, a woman had been at the heart of the conflict.

Their mother.

Just as they had been the first Christmas after she left, all the signs were there. Light arms. Floating stomach. Numb face. Metallic mouth.

"You have no idea what you're talking about." This had been Remy's line on that bleak gray morning twenty-two years ago. Now it was Law's.

"You're actually going to stand there and defend her?" Law's, now spoken by Remy.

"I'm *not* defending her," Law said, breaking the cycle. He wasn't. Couldn't. But he also couldn't stand to hear his brother talk about her this way.

"She came here, screwed you, then screwed *us*." He swung his hand out over the railing, sweeping the distillery and everyone in it into his accusation. "Whether you want to admit that to yourself is on you."

Law paused to gather his thoughts before he spoke.

"*Brother*, you and I have weathered a lot together.

So I want you to know that I mean what I'm about to say with the best possible intentions."

"I'm listening," Remy said with a subtle incline of his head.

"You ever say anything like that about her again… we're going to have a problem."

"We already *have* a problem."

Law turned to look out over the distillery, unable to confront the naked pain contorting features so similar to his own. "We'll go with one of the other offers for the expansion—"

"It's not about the goddamn expansion and you know it." Remy's growl ripped through the tense, pungent air.

He didn't just *know* it, he had carried the weight of that knowledge in his bones.

Guilt.

Guilt for trusting Augustin when Remy expressed hesitation.

Guilt for not listening to Remy when he tried to warn him about Jessica.

Guilt for the years of life his brother had lost because of Law's own stupidity.

Remy stepped into his peripheral vision, arms folded across his chest as he stood at Law's side. Together, they stared out at the row of gleaming stills. It had been nothing short of alchemy. Turning their blood, sweat and tears into copper, then liquor, then gold.

"You know that I wouldn't change anything about that night, right?" He asked this not with vitriol or triumph, but with a quiet, brotherly consolation.

Remy didn't need to tell him which.

The night they ran away.

Or tried to, anyway.

Law had been sixteen, Remy eighteen. The arbitrary line dividing adolescence and adulthood somewhere between them.

Robichaud's Salvage.

They'd hit this place before, but only for parts.

It had been Law's idea to break into the office to see if they could find enough cash to buy them both bus tickets to Virginia instead of burning through the little they'd managed to squirrel away.

They had gained access to the boxy trailer without incident. Remy set to work on picking the lock to the drawer in Blue Robichaud's desk where they'd seen him stash money. Law kept an eye on the yard until that eye spied the centerfold stuck to the wall just next to the ancient AC unit.

Law had been so mesmerized that he didn't notice the beam of the flashlight pouring through the blinds until Remy grabbed him by the scruff of the neck and shoved him toward the window at the opposite end of the trailer.

Despite Law's protests, his older but smaller brother had practically shoved him out of it, spitting one word at him as he hit the red dirt.

"Run."

He had.

Leaving Remy there to take the blame.

"Even though it cost you five years of your life?" Law asked.

"Especially because of that," Remy said, glancing over at him. "After I got out, I ran around crazy, trying to make up for all I'd missed, and do you know what it taught me?"

"I'm sure you're going to tell me," Law said.

Remy placed a hand on the railing. "There's no outrunning a past like ours, brother. Not with booze and bikes. Not with business plans and billionaire heiresses. Until you square with what's in your blood, you'll always be that scared boy from the bayou, begging for a seat at the table."

He was silent a moment.

"I'm going to the reception," Law said. He had known it the second he'd read her note, but his brother's words had only served to solidify his decision.

"Don't suppose it would do me any good to talk you out of it."

Law shook his head. "Not a bit."

"Whatever happens…" Remy began.

"It's you and me," Law finished.

Just as they had so many times and in so many contexts, they grasped hands, muscle memory taking their fingers through movements they hadn't performed in years.

They finished by clapping each other on the back and Law set off to the house to throw a few essentials into a bag.

The suit, he'd buy in New York City. Something more befitting the kind of wedding reception he suspected it would be.

And he would have his seat at the table.

Because he needed to know. He needed to look Marlowe in the eye and ask the questions swarming in his brain.

About the audit. About the investment.

About all of it.

Positive.

In almost any other circumstance in Marlowe Kane's world, this word was a welcome one.

Positive accounting theory.

Positive debt-to-equity ratio.

Positive circularization.

Glancing at the slim white stick in her trembling hand, she squeezed her eyelids shut so hard that a screen of swirling red appeared behind them. When she opened them again, the image in the small, rectangular window near the base of the middle of the stick remained the same. A small plus sign accompanied by three letters in all caps.

YES.

YES, she was pregnant.

The bathroom shrank as creeping gray fog pinholed her vision to a single spot. She sat hard on the marble step leading up to the giant soaking tub opposite a picture window. Beyond the pristine glass, millions of people went about their Saturday rituals in downtown Manhattan, not a single one of them knowing that, nearby, a life had been irrevocably changed.

Hers.

Some desperate sector of her brain attempted to remind her of friends who had received a false-positive result. Over-the-counter pregnancy tests weren't infallible, after all.

The glimmer of hope died out as a wave of nausea rolled her stomach and flooded her mouth with saliva. She catapulted herself from the step and lurched toward the commode, violently evicting the few sips of celebratory mimosa she'd managed to keep down since this morning.

This had become a relatively new ritual over the past few days. One that Marlowe had initially convinced herself must be the result of stress from the impending nuptials. Which was why she had sneaked away from the St. Pierre Hotel this morning to pick up a pregnancy test, purely to put her mind at ease so she could focus on her brother's wedding.

Or so she'd thought.

When the onslaught passed, Marlowe closed the lid and rested her cheek against the tile wall.

What the hell was she going to do?

The question now applied equally to the rest of the day…and the rest of her life.

With the ceremony mere hours away, she couldn't remain molded around a toilet, complete with a gold flusher, in the presidential suite in the St. Pierre Hotel.

On the other side of the door, Arlington Banks—soon to become Arlington Banks-Kane—and her bridesmaids chattered happily as they changed into their gowns.

Soon it would be time for pictures.

"Everything okay in there?"

Marlowe recognized the warm, plummy voice of Kassidy Nichols, Arlie's best friend and maid of honor. Though Kassidy had been only one year ahead of her at Lennox Finch Preparatory Academy, Marlowe remembered watching her rack up a laundry list of academic achievements despite frequently bending the rules. Always ready with a clever explanation for an unexcused absence, Kassidy had emanated an effortless cool that Marlowe had secretly admired from a respectful distance.

"Yes," she called a little too insistently. "Be right out."

A beat of silence.

"All right."

Lowering her head, she began to do her least favorite kind of math.

She'd barely had anything she could consider a cycle since she'd gotten her birth control implant several years ago, so she couldn't rely upon that particular clue to calculate the likely window of conception.

What she did know was that she'd been with only two men in the last year, and those encounters had been separated by a span of two months.

Which meant that in terms of the father, there was really only one option.

Law.

Heat baked her already-clammy cheeks, prompting a fresh wave of sweat to bloom at her hairline and her neck. Slowly, she reached for the gilded bar holding plush hand towels and helped herself to rise.

With the careful, wading gait of a drunk, Marlowe padded over to the vanity and forced herself to meet her own eyes in the large marble-bordered mirror.

You are pregnant with Law Renaud's baby.

An illicit thrill quivered in her still-roiling middle.

Her hand floated to her belly, still flat beneath the silk fabric of the matching sage-green robes they had all donned for "getting ready" pictures. Staring at her fingers, she imagined the small seed unfolding somewhere in the warm darkness beneath them.

Pregnant.

It didn't seem like a word.

It seemed like a lens. Instantly altering the entire world viewed through its warping gaze.

A quiet tapping at the door startled Marlowe out of her rosy, light-headed haze and she quickly grabbed the pregnancy test and shoved it into the vintage silk pouch bearing the spa-themed bridesmaids' gifts Arlie had handed out that morning.

"Can I come in?" Kassidy asked in a voice low enough as to sound conspiratorial.

Quickly blotting the sheen from her already-wilting makeup, Marlowe tossed the tissue and opened the door. Kassidy hurried inside, shut the door behind her and placed a large toiletry bag on the vanity's gleaming counter.

Examining their reflections in the mirror, Marlowe couldn't help but notice the startling contrast in the figures they cut.

Kassidy, a gently sloping masterpiece of perfectly proportional curves.

Marlowe, taller, a sharp-edged economy of lines.

How will a pregnancy change that? How will a pregnancy change me?

Already, her mind had begun to tumble questions like clothes in a dryer.

Kassidy unzipped the bag and began pulling out various contents. "Okay, level with me. What are we dealing with? Hangover, food poisoning, anxiety attack… morning sickness?"

Only when she caught the wicked glint in Kassidy's eye did she realize Arlie's friend had been teasing about the last option. Unfortunately, the realization didn't come quickly enough to keep the blood from draining from Marlowe's face.

"Holy shit." Kassidy put a warm hand on Marlowe's elbow and guided her to the velvet stool parked in front of the vanity. "You're gray as a goddamn ghost."

Once seated, the small black spots at the corners of Marlowe's vision thankfully ceased their relentless cartwheeling.

"I...forgot to eat breakfast this morning." The lie tasted metallic on her tongue. "I'm just a little dizzy."

"I'm on it." Turning to her bag, Kassidy unzipped the side pocket and pulled out a protein bar and a single-serving bottle of an electrolyte-recovery drink. "Down them," she ordered.

Marlowe did as told, relieved when the electric-blue beverage slid down her throat like liquid silk, cooling the acidic burn. The protein bar tasted mostly like peanut butter–flavored sawdust but didn't cause her stomach to roil upon contact.

"Thank you," she said around a mouthful. "You didn't...*hear* me, did you?"

"Not a peep." Kassidy fished in her bag and came out with an orange prescription-pill bottle.

"Then how did you—"

"Know you were in here dry heaving?" The flawless tawny skin of Kassidy's forehead creased as she squinted at first one plastic sandwich bag containing various over-the-counter medications, then another. "I felt it. I swear this maid-of-honor shit has given me some kind of matrimonial-crisis, psychic radar."

Draining the last of her drink, Marlowe crumpled the bar wrapper, tucked it in the empty bottle and dropped it in the waste bin. "Do you have an entire pharmacy in there?"

"Only certain pharmacological aids I thought might come in handy on a day like today. I've got Tylenol, Rolaids, vitamin V..."

"Vitamin V?" Marlowe asked.

"Valium." Kassidy's full lips quirked at one corner. "Which I've only been tempted to slip into the wedding planner's latte on four separate occasions this morning.

If he were any higher strung, the harpist could play the processional on *him*."

Marlowe's pallid lips stretched in a smile, grateful to think about anything other than the catastrophic consequences looming like a dirigible overhead.

"You want something for nausea?" Kassidy rattled another prescription-pill bottle in Marlowe's direction.

She'd opened her mouth to say something in the neighborhood of "please, God, yes" when it occurred to her that she had no idea what medications may or may not be harmful to a pregnancy.

"Ginger chews?" Kassidy asked, a small bag swinging from her perfectly manicured fingers. "Vegan, organic and all-natural."

"Sure," Marlowe said.

After dropping the small twist-wrapped drop into Marlowe's hand, Kassidy grabbed a handful and set them on the counter. "Extras."

This small act of care loosened the tension knotted like a baseball between her shoulders.

"Arlie chose wisely." Marlowe swept the chews into her bridesmaid's bag, trying not to think how they might nestle against a particular object within, emitting a sonar-like pulse in her awareness. "You're an amazing maid of honor."

Kassidy treated her with a blindingly gorgeous grin. "You expected any different?"

"Not for a second." Hands on the cool marble counter, Marlowe began to rise. "I think I'm okay to go get changed."

Her ascent was gently halted by Kassidy's hand on her shoulder. "Not until I fix your face, you're not."

"I think it may be beyond repair at this point." Turning to the mirror, Marlowe assessed her pallid skin, less than delighted by the slightly bilious undertone of the shadows beneath her eyes.

"For lesser mortals, maybe. Hold, please." Kassidy swept out the door and returned moments later with a chic, dusty-blue case that resembled a miniature version of a vintage suitcase.

This bleary, inconsequential memory produced a longing for her mother's familiar, maternal presence so acute that it threatened to steal her breath.

She'd had a mother once.

A quiet, kind soul with jade green eyes like her brother's and pale hair like Marlowe's.

A wise, warm woman who would patiently listen to her inconsequential adolescent woes and allow them the gravitas of a thoughtful answer.

What sage advice might her mother offer about her current predicament were she still alive to give it?

"*Allll* right." Kassidy tipped up Marlowe's chin with a light touch and peered at her face, assessing the damage. "We have our marching orders." She unlatched the box and set out an array of cosmetics ranging from concealer to waterproof mascara.

Thankfully, Marlowe had had the foresight to apply it already this morning, as she had been oddly weepy in the past couple of weeks. Yet another detail that made much more sense in light of her recent discovery.

"Arlie and Samuel," Kassidy sighed. Leaning forward, she emanated a delicate cloud of vanilla and sandalwood as she gently patted a makeup sponge beneath each of Marlowe's closed eyes. "After all this time. Who'd have thought?"

Marlowe certainly hadn't. Hadn't thought Samuel was likely to marry at all, as Kane Foods had been the prime recipient of his slavish devotion for years. Much less that, if he did, Mason would be his best man. After all the years they'd spent alternately ignoring and annoying one another, the rapid shift to complete concord had been a little dizzying.

And lonely.

"Crazy," Marlowe said. "Isn't it?"

Uncurling her hand, Marlowe blindly unwrapped the ginger drop and popped it in her mouth. The spicy heat quickly blotted the cloying aromas of leftover brunch from her sinuses. Her throat warmed and her stomach steadied.

Magic.

"Do you believe in soul mates?" Kassidy asked. She had moved on from the makeup sponge to a large, fluffy brush that she dipped in a container of loose powder, knocking the excess off on a tissue before gliding it softly over Marlowe's face.

She felt her shoulders begin to melt away from her ears as the featherlight touch moved over her forehead, her cheeks, her jaw.

It was the most relaxed she had felt since…since it didn't bear thinking about.

"If there is such a thing, the odds are one in ten thousand of you ever finding them." Her voice was thick and slow, a yawn aching at the base of her throat. "Provided they're born in roughly the same age bracket. If not, the odds just go down from there."

Kassidy snorted under her breath. "I see the romance of it all is getting to you, too."

The delicious sensation of the brush ceased and was replaced by tickling strokes along her brow bones.

"Do *you* believe in soul mates?"

There was a clatter as Kassidy dropped something into the case. "I believe in energy. And that everyone vibes at a different level. I think when you meet someone whose energy naturally matches yours, the resulting attraction can *feel* like a soul mate."

"Huh," Marlowe said.

"Same thing applies to love at first sight," Kassidy continued. "I think it's not love so much as an energetically induced dopamine-and-norepinephrine speedball."

Flashes of Law arrogantly leaning against the wall across the ballroom appeared on the screens of her eyelids. "What if you're immediately attracted to someone physically but can't stand them once they open their mouth?"

"Mmm...mmm...mmm," Kassidy hummed through her closed lips.

"What?" Marlowe asked.

"Scenario like that, one of two things is going to happen." A mint-scented exhalation warmed Marlowe's cheeks as Kassidy repaired her eyeliner with a steady hand.

"I'm listening." This was only half-true. Marlowe's mind had already begun to wander. Out of the presidential suite, out of the hotel, out of the city. All the way back to a quiet, leafy clearing where she'd watered the earth with her tears while in the circle of Law's arms.

"You're either going to have a damn good time that ends with blocking of numbers and burning of all artifacts or pick out a house in the suburbs and start researching local Montessori preschools."

Preschools.

Schools where children sang songs, ate snacks, took naps.

Could she picture herself there? Her BMW parked in the curving line of cars waiting to pick up the chaotic flood of tiny humans spilling through the doors at the end of the school day?

"All right," Kassidy announced. "I think you're officially keepsake-photo ready."

Marlowe opened her eyes and glanced at herself in the mirror. Kassidy had injected life into her lips and cheeks, utterly eradicating the sickly pallor. She'd even made her eyelids appear less puffy and sleep-deprived.

"You are some kind of fairy godmother, right?" she asked.

"The kind that enjoys dirty martinis and even dirtier weekends with a very talented prosecutor from the state attorney's office." Taking a step back, Kassidy examined her handiwork, a slight frown tugging at her mouth. "There's still something— Wait! I know." While she rooted around in her Mary Poppins-esque bag of tricks, Marlowe quickly popped another chew into her mouth.

"Bingo!" Soft, fragrant fingers brushed the hair from Marlowe's temple, securing it with a glittering art deco comb. A succession of triangular gemstone-encrusted chevrons echoed the shape of her jaw.

"Circa 1930s." Kassidy gave Marlowe's shoulder a squeeze. "But clearly it was made for you."

An urgent rap on the door preceded Charlotte's smoothly professional announcement that the wedding planner would be arriving in fifteen minutes to escort them downstairs to the rooftop venue for the ceremony.

You can take the girl out of the corporate office...

"Should we get out there and slip into our backup dancer attire?" Kassidy asked. "If we're not dressed when the planner arrives, he's liable to have a stroke."

Marlowe filled her lungs with a deep breath and stood, grateful when the cool marble tiles remained anchored beneath her feet. "Let's."

Once Kassidy had exited, Marlowe lifted her handbag from the counter. Pulling the drawstring wide, she stared at the pregnancy test, half of her expecting to find it negative after all, and the last fifteen minutes all just a bizarre, hallucinatory dream.

The plus mark remained—if anything, an even darker pink than it had been.

Though she quickly drew the bag closed, the perpendicular lines burned in the small darkness of the bag like a glyph.

Plus.

Marlowe *plus* one.

Marlowe plus one huge, life-altering secret.

Thirteen

The grand ballroom of the St. Pierre Hotel had been transformed into a glittering autumn fairy forest for Samuel and Arlie's reception. Crystal and candles adorning every available surface. Enchanted and intimate despite the hall's cavernous size. Marlowe collapsed into the chair at her appointed table, feeling like she'd just crossed the finish line of a marathon. Miraculously, she'd made it through the entire ceremony without needing to dash down the side aisle to vomit into one of the floral arrangements. She hadn't been quite as lucky when it came to holding in her tears.

First, exiting the bathroom and seeing Arlie in her vintage Dior wedding gown. Second, watching Samuel, tuxedo clad and handsome, fighting emotion as Mason—filling in for Arlie's late father—escorted her down the aisle. Third, looking out into the sea of faces and finding *her* father caught in an unguarded moment, gazing past the dais and into mental terrain that made his eyes crinkle in the corners as she hadn't seen in years.

Since then, her eyes had leaked intermittently throughout the evening.

If it wasn't for the handkerchief she had tucked in her bridesmaid bag, she'd likely resemble a Monet by this point.

Now, if she could at least get through dinner, she could melt into the crowd when the dancing started and retreat to her room, where she could panic about her life in peace.

By the time the entire wedding party was seated at the head table, Marlowe wasn't so sure about her chances.

Large, untraditionally round and positioned at the front of the ballroom, the eight-top table afforded the newlyweds an opportunity to interact intimately with the wedding party. Only the chair next to Marlowe's remained conspicuously empty, waiting to be occupied by her father.

If he ever finished skimming from table to table like an oversize water bug.

An impeccably groomed server arrived with a bottle of chilled sauvignon blanc from the Kane family's own Willow Creek winery to accompany the first course. Marlowe allowed him to pour lest her out-of-character refusal raise any eyebrows, but sipped at ice water instead. Still, she couldn't help but look longingly at the pale gold liquid quickly filming the crystal with a fine mist of condensation.

Are you okay? Arlie mouthed, leaning around the tall trumpet vase of the centerpiece. Having changed out of her formal wedding gown and into a more dance-friendly, but equally stunning, lace evening dress, the bride had seemed oddly attentive, ocean-blue eyes concerned as they took in Marlowe's untouched wine.

Short answer?

No.

She was decidedly *not* okay.

The cacophony of smells that marked the beginning of the six-course meal had woken her nausea.

Giving her newly minted sister-in-law a quick nod, she lifted her fork and made a show of poking through the salad of artfully arranged crisped kale and roasted root vegetables. She speared a bite of crispy sweet potato and chewed slowly, encouraged that her throat didn't immediately seize.

When the table had made a decent dent in the first course, the salads were cleared and soups set down in service so synchronized, it could have been a competitive sport.

Marlowe sniffed at the steam curling up from the silky marigold liquid dappled with olive oil and strewn with microgreens.

Cream of pumpkin.

It had been Samuel's favorite of the recipes Arlie's late mother had always included in the fall retinue when cooking for their family.

Damned if the thought didn't sting tears to Marlowe's eyes.

Again.

She blinked them away quickly, fixing a grateful smile on her face and looking to Arlie.

Who had frozen with her soupspoon halfway to her open mouth.

Fine hairs lifted on Marlowe's neck as chill bumps danced over her bared arms.

All at once, she *knew*.

Even before the scent of resiny soap, wood smoke and clean linen reached her nose.

Before the ponderously deep voice rumbled into her ear.

Law Renaud was behind her.

Awareness traveled around the table like a shock wave, moving from Samuel to Mason, to Charlotte, to Kassidy, back to Arlie, whose eyes seemed to travel upward for a small eternity.

"Evening," he said, by way of greeting.

One word.

One *single* word and Marlowe felt her already-sensitive nipples hardening against her bra as a warmth spilled through her. Her body's pathetically Pavlovian reaction to his proximity, even after the time they'd been apart. She didn't dare turn to look at him lest she burst into spontaneous flame.

The table's collective gaze shifted to Marlowe, expectant of a forthcoming introduction.

With her heart knocking against her ribs, she frantically evaluated her options and seized upon the only one she thought capable of defusing a potentially awkward scene.

"Would you excuse us for a moment?" She began to rise but was thwarted by a warm, heavy hand on her shoulder. Her bare skin tingled and sang with memory.

"No need to get up." Law pulled out the empty chair next to hers and settled into it. "I don't see any reason we can't talk right here."

When she caught the first flash of him in her peripheral vision, her sister-in-law's midbite pause made much more sense.

To see his huge, hulking frame in a midnight blue, beautifully cut suit, complete with coordinated vest and tie, was as dazzling as it was jarring. Paired with the dark hair combed back from his brutal features and the goatee framing his wicked mouth, Law looked more like a sexy mob-movie villain than a wedding guest.

"What are you doing here?" she asked in a low, harsh sideways whisper.

His dark brows lowered in a scowl of confusion. "You invited me."

To hear such disorienting words against the sweetly singing music of a string quartet proved intensely disorienting. Marlowe looked to her brothers, always her anchor, only to find matching expressions of piqued bemusement on both their faces.

What the *hell* was going on here?

"I have no idea what you're talking about," she said, directing her words to him but her gaze toward the centerpiece.

"This." Law reached into his suit coat and produced a creamy card, holding it out to her.

She recognized it as the invitation Arlie had insisted on mailing to her despite Marlowe's protestations that she could just hand it over and save on the postage. On the back, she found a note.

Please come. We need to talk.
—MK

MK.
Confusion gave way to realization with a bright crystalline *ping* inside her head.

"What. Did. You. Do?" She shot the words like bullets in her brother's direction.

Mason held his hands up in the don't-shoot gesture he often employed when shooting was *exactly* what the situation called for. "Before you freak out—"

"I didn't send this to you." Her fist closed like a vise, crumpling the card, thrusting it toward Law. "My brother Mason just made it seem like I did."

"Technically, I didn't make it seem like anything." Mason nodded his thanks to the attendant who removed his empty soup bowl. "He just saw the initials and assumed it was you."

"You've done some idiotic shit in your day, but this? You just randomly send an invitation to Samuel and Arlie's wedding to *Law Renaud*?"

"So, that's who our mystery guest is." Kassidy, seated on the other side of Law, extended her hand. "Kassidy Nichols. Maid of honor."

Law folded his around it. "Law Renaud. Fucking confused."

Mason sat back in his chair, resting a hand on Charlotte's thigh beneath the table. "It wasn't random at all, I assure you," he said, picking up the thread of her question.

At last, she had processed her shock enough to notice just how *un*-shocked everyone else at the table appeared. Even Kassidy's use of the term *mystery guest* took on all-new meaning.

"You *knew* about this?" Disbelief crushed the breath from Marlowe's lungs. She glared at Samuel, then at the ladies at her brothers' sides. "You *all* knew about this?"

Charlotte looked to Arlie, who looked to Kassidy. A visual relay race, a baton of contrition being passed.

Beads of sweat broke out on Marlowe's forehead and upper lip. Her silk gown suctioned to her body, clinging like an unwelcome second skin.

"I cannot believe…cannot even *begin* to fathom that you would—" Her brain skipped like a scratched record as she struggled to speak, her breath hitching.

This was, of course, her fault.

Her fault, because not a single soul at this table knew what had truly happened during her time at 4 Thieves. Or what had happened since.

Mason had made an effort when she'd returned, an obvious bid to make up for his previous fraternal neglect.

He had asked the right questions, made the right noises when she'd offered her very watered-down answers. Yes, she'd found Law charming. Yes, she'd enjoyed her time there. Yes, she might consider seeing him again, if work ever died down.

Shockingly, it never had.

A familiar weight pressed between her shoulder blades, another at her collarbones. Straightening her posture. Drawing her down from the dizzying heights of her panic. Law's voice rumbled in her ear. "Breathe."

"I have a fan." Kassidy hoisted the silk bridesmaid's bag onto the table and began to paw through it, finally growing so frustrated that she upended it onto the table.

Marlowe watched as the contents spilled out in slow motion. Face powder. Lipstick.

A pregnancy test.

The bright pink plus sign and blocky *YES* clearly visible.

Somewhere in the shuffle between the endless rounds of post-ceremony pictures, cocktail hour and reception, Kassidy must have grabbed her bag by accident. Of all the ridiculously unfortunate, cosmically twisted things to have happened at her brother's wedding, it had been this.

Had this been any other table, the contents of her bag would have been quickly shoved back in the bag, embarrassed apologies offered.

It would have to be…discussed.

They all stared at it with faces wiped blank by shock as it sat there next to the copper charger, like a hand grenade. Seconds from blowing her orderly life into flaming oblivion.

The world around her seemed to shrink. The hum of conversation amplifying to abrasive quacking. Facets of cut crystal strobing candlelight in a dizzying whirl. The ballroom's soaring ceiling hunkering like a circus tent.

Fear.

Great gouts of it, transforming the moment into a horror carnival.

Arlie broke the silence first. Hand flying to her mouth with a gasp, she looked from the stick to her maid of honor. "Kass?"

"Oh no. *Hell* no." Kassidy's riot of onyx curls bounced as she vehemently shook her head and shoved everything into the bag. "Not my monkey, not my circus."

Twin expressions of worry leaped onto her brothers' faces as they turned to their partners, talking over each other in their haste.

"Y-you're not—" Mason stuttered.

"Are you—" Samuel began.

"I am," Marlowe answered, unwilling to let herself be outed by the process of elimination.

Beside her, Law's entire body jerked. One large, quick jolt. Like he'd taken a bullet.

She turned. Made herself look at him full in the face for the first time since his arrival.

He didn't speak. Didn't blink. He only studied her with a galaxy of questions spinning in the depths of his dark eyes, the chief among them etched clearly on his face.

Mine?

She nodded.

"I found out this morning. Right before we came down for the ceremony. Which is why I didn't have time to… I had planned on—"

"Perhaps," Samuel interrupted, clearing his throat, "this might be a discussion better continued elsewhere?" Following the flick of his eyes, she noted that their father had reached the next table, his back turned to them.

"Go," Arlie urged. "If anyone asks, we'll tell them there was a wedding-toast emergency."

Law rose as she did. Willing her legs not to wobble, she attempted to walk like a woman *not* visualizing a pirate's plank stretching out ahead of her.

As she passed, Samuel captured her clammy hand, gave it a gentle squeeze. Marlowe squeezed in return, grateful for this one, small gesture of solidarity.

They wove their way through the tables and out of the ballroom, down a lushly carpeted hall, and across the white-and-black chessboard lobby floor to the already-open elevator.

The brushed brass doors sealed them in, and they were alone.

Marlowe Kane, billionaire heiress.

And Law Renaud, father of her unborn child.

Fourteen

Could this elevator go any slower?

Law stared at the glowing button for the thirty-ninth floor, irritated at the numbers lazily ticking by as they rode upward. Eight, nine, nine and a half…

He fought the urge to pace like the caged animal he was.

Trapped with a woman whose proximity set his blood racing. A woman who had quite literally taken his god-damn breath away.

He'd lurked in the entry to the ballroom when he first arrived, scanning the tables, wanting to know exactly where she was heading before he exposed himself to the scrutiny of the gilded, glittering crowd.

When he spotted her seated alone at a table, the sight had mule-kicked the air from his lungs.

She was exquisite. So much more beautiful than he'd even remembered.

Her lips fuller, her eyes a brighter blue, her hair gleaming a brighter, pale gold. The elegance of her every line, plane and angle aglow.

Before he could work up the nerve to take a single step toward her, he'd had to down two shots at the bar.

After what unfolded in the aftermath, he was damn glad he had.

I am.

His heart hadn't stopped pounding since Marlowe had spoken these words. His stomach had rollercoaster-floated up into his rib cage and fallen just as hard when he realized he had no reason to assume her pregnancy had anything to do with him.

Then he'd looked in her eyes, and even before her nod, he knew.

He *knew.*

Neither of them had spoken since they left the table. As if in agreement that what they had to say couldn't be said in a hallway or elevator.

Not that Law had any idea what *to* say.

He'd been leveled by this bombshell, left picking through rubble of desperate questions and coming back to the same two.

Has she decided if she wants to carry the pregnancy?
Do I want her to?

Their elevator car glided to a stop, his freedom from the suffocating luxe cube announced with a musical *ting.*

Canine-loyal lust snaked into his gut as he watched the silk dress dance across her ass as she walked, flashing him the curve only to conceal it again. The back dipped low enough to reveal that she couldn't be wearing a bra—at least, not one of the conventional variety. Damned if that didn't fan the very inconvenient flames.

She paused about halfway, fishing in her bag for a key card that she swiped at a small black panel on the door.

He followed her in and suddenly wished the accommodations were *more* luxurious. A suite would have been nice. Preferably with a separate sitting area where they could talk far, far away from the very large, very sumptuous bed parked right in the middle of the room.

"Make yourself at home." She stepped out of her high-heeled shoes and dropped the key card on the entryway table, tossing her bag beside it.

His eyes lingered on the green silk for a beat, feeling a sudden urge to excavate the now-infamous contents. To hold the test in his hand.

Pregnant.

Even though she'd been on birth control. He hadn't asked what kind, but was certain that if Marlowe trusted it, it probably fell into the over-99-percent-effective category.

Lord, but that less than 1 percent could bite you in the ass.

Marlowe walked over to the sprawling polished-wood cabinet beneath the wall-mounted flat-screen TV. She crouched to open the doors at its center, revealing an extensive minibar.

"Something to drink?"

Law hesitated, hating himself a little when he answered, "If you're having one."

Because he knew exactly what he was doing. Trying to guess the answer to question one before it had been asked aloud.

His chest tightened when her hand moved toward a half-sized bottle of vodka and released when her fingers closed over a bottle of Perrier instead.

Shit.

One step closer to an answer on his end.

"Does this count as a drink?" She twisted open the cap and poured the effervescent contents into one of the rocks glasses provided in the cabinet.

"Seeing as that little bottle probably costs twenty dollars, I'm going to go with yes," he answered.

"Then what's your choice?"

As badly as he wanted—no, *needed*—courage for this conversation, Law wasn't about to drink in front of her if she'd decided not to.

"They have any nonaggressive water in there?" he asked.

"Artesian spring water from the Swiss Alps?" The bottle she held up was long, sleek and made of actual glass. "Or would the gentleman prefer to take it directly from the tap?" she asked with a wry twist of her lips.

"Artesian," he said. "But only because it would be rude to let you be pretentious all on your own."

"In a glass or from the bottle?"

He raised an eyebrow at her. "You're telling me people really pour water from a glass bottle into a glass *glass*?"

"Some people do, yes." Deciding for him, she opened the bottle and tipped it into a matching rocks glass. "It's an entirely different sensory experience."

"Some people like *you*?"

They were engaged in the smallest talk possible, but he felt relieved to let it burn off some of the tension.

"You've got me pegged all wrong." Marlowe handed him the water. "I never would have opened the minibar in the first place."

"That so?"

"I'm a corporate comptroller, Law. I object to them on principle. The idea of paying fifteen dollars for Snickers offends my very soul." She clinked her glass against his and sipped.

"Tonight is an exception?"

She aimed a pointed look at him. "Don't you think it should be?"

With that, she had steered them straight to the proverbial elephant.

Marlowe exhaled a long breath and sank onto the white leather bench at the foot of the bed.

Opting for the only other non-bed-related surface, Law lowered himself into a reading chair in the adjacent corner.

"So, Law Renaud." She offered him a wan smile. "What the hell are we going to do?"

Rolling his glass between his palms, he studied the subtle quatrefoil patterns in the deeply piled carpet. "You don't think there's any chance the test could be wrong?"

She blew out a gust of air. "If it weren't for the fact that I spent the entire morning of my brother's wedding and several days leading up to it heaving my guts repeatedly, I might be more inclined to entertain that as a possibility."

A sympathetic twinge tugged at his stomach. In

terms of his least favorite experiences, vomiting was right up there with road rash. "I'm sorry," he said.

"Not your fault." Her shoulders jerked upward in a shrug. "I mean, it is, I guess, but...not on purpose."

Law bit the inside of his cheek. Anything to keep his mind from wandering back to the memory—*memories*—associated with his part of their predicament. "So that would be...what?" He made a show of counting, pretending he hadn't already done it the moment he'd found out. "Seven weeks?"

"Nine," she corrected.

"Nine?" His brows drew together before he could stop his face from registering surprise.

"It's actually calculated from the first day of your—" Pausing, she assessed him with a questioning look. "Do you really want to hear about all this?"

"I do," he said and meant it.

"The first day of your cycle is where the nine-month term begins, even though ovulation typically happens somewhere in the twelve-to-fourteen-day window and you're only fertile for a twelve-to-twenty-four-hour period after it happens. Which, it shouldn't if you have an IUD that isn't totally useless." An edge of bitterness laced the final element of her explanation.

"So you're over two months, then," he said.

Leaning back on her palms, she crossed one leg over the other. Her gown flared, the slit crawling farther up her long, lean thigh.

Law's knuckles whitened around his rocks glass. He remembered how silky that precise terrain had been. How it had shuddered when he traced upward to the curve of her hip bone, then lower.

"I would need to get an ultrasound to be absolutely

certain, but working from the date of the, uh, audit, it would just about have to be in that range."

The audit.

Just about have to be...

These words gnawed holes of doubt into his head, allowing an ugly, suspicious thought to seep in.

She screwed you, then she screwed us over.

The refrain came to him, not in Remy's voice but his father's. Because Zap Renaud had surely been its author. Now it rose in him, too.

Reminding him of the questions he'd meant to ask before the revelation of her pregnancy had derailed him.

Questions that still needed answering.

"Do you think you might get one?" he asked.

"At the first available appointment at my OB-GYN's after I call them the second they open at 7:30 a.m. on Monday morning."

"Are they typically pretty busy, or...?" He trailed off, inviting her to volunteer the information he hadn't specifically requested.

"Are you asking because you'd like to know if it's going to be soon enough that you can come with me?" The gently teasing way she said this made him feel even more like a bastard.

It gave him more credit than he deserved. Because beneath his desire to be supportive, that oily voice still whispered.

Hear for yourself when conception took place. Then *you'll know how to feel about this.* If *there's anything to feel.*

"*If* that's something you wouldn't mind," he said, trying again to banish the other train of thought.

"Not at all," she said. "How long were you planning on staying in town?"

Law gazed into his glass. "Planning didn't much figure in."

"You were just going to show up and see what it was I wanted to talk to you about?" She drained the remaining water in her glass and set it aside.

"Not entirely," he admitted. "There was something I needed to talk with you about as well."

Her bare foot began a nervous jiggle. Though he tried desperately not to, Law followed the vibration up her calf where it rippled the silk of her dress and created a subtle answering quiver in her breasts. Definitely unrestrained. There could be no doubt now.

He bit down harder on his cheek.

"When that invitation from Mason arrived, it didn't show up alone." He studied her face, searching for some hint of recognition but finding only expectation.

Reaching into the pocket of his blazer, he pulled out a sheet of paper that had been folded into fourths.

"Your suit is just full of surprises tonight." She leaned forward to take it, fingers unfolding the stiff paper.

Law looked up at the exact second that her tired smile slid from its moorings.

The first page of the letter informing him of Kane Foods' formal cancellation of the investment proceedings fluttered from her hand to the bench beside her.

"Remy told me about the conversation you two had the morning you left. I know that your father sent you to 4 Thieves to find something that would allow him to undercut the original offer we'd discussed. To teach us a lesson."

Marlowe gaped at him, her skin turned alabaster white. Words failed to find their way out her parted lips.

This was not the scenario he'd rehearsed while the road hummed under his truck tires on the drive from Fincastle. Something had shifted in the hour since he'd valet-parked his car and stepped into the St. Pierre's lobby. Seeing Marlowe for the first time since the summer. Sitting next to her at the table. Looking into her eyes and knowing she carried a spark they'd created together.

In this small space of time, he had finally told himself the truth.

This was the only answer he'd really come for.

To know if he really was a fool. Still, that same silly boy creating in his head what only existed in his heart. Convincing himself they had shared something real. Something true.

"Whatever you decide to do about this pregnancy, I'll support you," he said. "I need you to understand that. But before I leave this room, I need you to know where I stand."

Marlowe sucked in a ragged breath and stood. One arm hugged across her breasts and the other around her middle, she walked to the wide window, giving him her back. He heard a watery sniffle.

Law rose from his chair and crossed the room, stopping far enough away to give her space but close enough to make sure she could hear him clearly. Because he wasn't sure he had the strength to do this twice.

"It's been two months since you left, and I *still* don't have you out of my system. I've done everything I possibly can to uproot this ridiculous, inconvenient attachment to you, and nothing has worked. Not when I got the news that Kane Foods was passing us over. The closest I've come is hearing from my own brother that you slept with me as some sort of smoke screen for your true motives." His jaw tightened, a reflexive re-action against laying himself bare. Forcing it to relax, he went on. "And then tonight, I spend one hour with you, and somehow, I forget. *That's* the kind of power you have over me."

She drew in a shaky breath and turned to him. Twin tear tracks silvered her cheeks below downcast eyes. "Law—"

He held up a hand. "Just let me get this all out and you'll never have to hear it again."

A sigh of surrender deflated her chest.

"If having a baby is something you decide you do want, I want to be there. I don't care what I have to do to make it happen. That's what *I* want."

God help him, he did want it. Even as he endured a life-flashing-before-your-eyes montage of all the rea-sons *not* to carry on the Renaud name. The generations of hurt and hardship. The betrayals and pain. All chan-neled through him.

Now, a chance to give a child of his own the things he'd lacked.

Protection. Guidance. Affection. Love.

Unconditional love. From a mother *and* a father.

Family.

He pressed a fist against the ache in his chest.

Almost there. Almost done.

"*But*, if Remy was right, and everything that hap-pened between us only happened because it was part of a plan, I need to hear you say it. I need to hear the words come from your mouth, because I think that's the only way I'll get it through my thick skull that I need to let you go."

He didn't flatter himself by pretending he was asking. He was begging. For absolution. For release. For an answer.

She hugged herself tighter as fresh tears slipped from her closed eyes, and Law could no longer hold himself back. Though he badly wanted to gather her against him and hold her until those tears dried, he settled for lightly cupping her jaw and tilting it upward.

"*Please*, Marlowe."

Her eyes lifted to meet his, her lips parted to speak.

Three bracing raps sounded on the door.

When it wasn't followed by the standard singsong announcement of housekeeping staff, they held the silence, hoping perhaps whoever it was would just go away.

Instead, a muffled beep announced a key card swiped across the sensor.

Law was halfway to the door before he realized he'd begun moving. "Hey!" he bellowed as the door began to swing inward. "This room is occupied."

"I'm very aware of that fact." The rich, resonant voice floated out of the shadowy entryway before the man stepped forward to meet it. Recognition landed in a one-two punch of limbic anger and adrenaline to Law's solar plexus as he looked into a face that had his fist twitching to make its acquaintance.

The face of Parker Kane.

Fifteen

Through her stinging, salt-crusted eyes, Marlowe looked from Law to her father and back again.

The day had left her so exhausted, so emotionally wrung out, so unbelievably spent, that even the idea of them accidentally encountering one another in her room at the St. Pierre failed to fill her with the proper amount of dread.

Currently, they were engaged in some sort of masculine staring contest. Law's blistering insurgence versus Parker Kane's frosty superiority. The former had about three inches of height and thirty pounds of brawn on his opponent. Where the Kane patriarch's power lived almost exclusively outside his physical body—as was often the case where emperors were concerned.

"Father," she said. "What are you doing here?"

Startlingly elegant in his bespoke tuxedo, he inclined

his neatly combed head. "I thought I would come to check on you. You've looked a little peaked all day and I couldn't conceive of what—other than illness—might keep you from your brother's wedding reception. I now see I lacked imagination." He raked a glance over Law, rigid as a toy soldier in his effort to maintain control.

Conceive.

God, she really wished he hadn't used that word. A very unwelcome addition to a response he'd managed to lace with insincere concern, a veiled critique, a subtle guilt trip *and* a gauntlet.

Impressive.

And effective.

As she'd learned long ago, just because she recognized her father's manipulation didn't mean she was immune to its consequences.

She *did* feel guilty for missing precious moments of this important occasion in her brother's life. But also hurt, angry, confused and terrified.

Terrified of what she knew she needed to say to both men squaring off before her. Terrified, because she knew the questions she needed to ask her father would answer Law's, and not in a way he would like.

Her stomach clenched, and she elected to resume her seat on the bench at the end of the bed, needing something solid beneath her. Once there, she picked up the folded page and held it out for her father's inspection. "Why was the intent to cancel the 4 Thieves investment kept a secret?"

He arched a silver-flecked brow at her but otherwise remained utterly still. "Is *this* why you crashed my son's reception?" he asked, shifting his attention in Law's direction to strike as swiftly as a snake. "In some sort of ill-advised bid to reverse my decision?"

"He's not crashing, Father," she said. "Mason invited him."

Parker Kane had the unique ability to make even a snort sound imperious. "We all know Mason is prone to impulsive—"

"*With* Samuel's permission," she interrupted. "Which is how I know that he was also unaware of the letter of cancellation. Samuel never would have allowed it if he had known. And within Kane Foods, Samuel knows everything. I'm asking again. *Why* did you have our lawyers covertly send this letter?"

"I seem to remember you specifically requesting that all matters pursuant to 4 Thieves be handled by a different party upon your return from the audit."

Seeing her window, Marlowe shot through it.

"An audit whose results suggested that 4 Thieves was worth significantly *more* than originally determined," she said, slapping the paper on the bench beside her. "That's why you wanted to cancel the investment. Isn't it? Because you knew you wouldn't be able to convince them to give you a larger chunk of the equity in exchange for your surprisingly generous investment?"

He sniffed, notching his chin up in the haughty manner she had tried and failed to school herself out of when on the receiving end of discomfort.

"I was not at all confident that the figures you reported were—"

"Don't pretend I don't know what I'm talking about." Fueled by a cocktail of pregnancy hormones and heady adrenaline, she shot to her feet. "You know that I'm damn good at structuring findings in your favor, because I've done it before."

Deafening silence. No longer a hyperbolic description.

Now was the part where Law would turn on the heel of his dress shoe and walk out of the room. Her life. Taking every wonderful, achingly beautiful, completely undeserved thing with him.

Across that endless wall of nothing, she searched Law's face.

Blank. Flat. Expressionless.

She had no idea what he was thinking. Or if she'd have the chance to explain exactly how she'd done what she'd done at her father's request.

Never in a way that officially crossed legal boundaries.

Ethical boundaries, on the other hand...

"I think that's the real reason you wanted back out of this, isn't it?" she asked. "Not because of anything 4 Thieves did. Because of what I didn't."

"Marlowe." Her father had always had a way of pronouncing her name that made it sound lavish and frivolous. All dripping *R* and overfed *O*. "I think the day's excitement has you a little overwrought. Perhaps you should stay here and rest after all."

"Don't." The bass rumble of Law's voice startled her. Up to this point, he'd been a sentinel, silently watching. Now he took a step closer, fingers curling into his palms.

The softness that had crept into her father's eyes vanished abruptly. "Don't *what*?"

"Don't dismiss her like that." He folded his arms across his massive chest, his biceps mounding beneath the arms of his jacket. "She asked you a question. Answer it."

The air had solidified into concrete, impossible to pull into her lungs. Never in her life had she seen a man—or anyone, for that matter—speak to her father this way.

Parker Kane may have lacked several inches in stature, but he still managed to look down on Law.

"I'm still not certain why it is you're here." *Here* may have been her hotel room in principle, but definitely planet Earth by his inflection.

"Because I'm pregnant with his child."

Her father's head jerked back as if a drink had been thrown in his face. He blinked several times in quick succession as his usually hale complexion turned a waxy gray.

This wasn't the way she'd imagined it. Back when she used to imagine such things. Neil had been part of the scenario then. There by her side as she presented her father with a succession of items until he guessed. A box of his favorite cigars, an application to Harvard—his alma mater—and a miniature polo mallet.

She had tried so hard to picture what his face might look like when happily surprised.

This certainly wasn't it.

Quite the opposite, in fact.

"This is a recent discovery, I take it?"

"This morning," she said.

Her father seemed to take comfort from this fact. "I know this may seem like a catastrophic event," he said in almost a conciliatory tone. "But there are still many options available to you once you've decided."

"I've decided already," she said.

Law's arms fell away from his torso. Their gazes met and held.

"I'm going to have the baby."

"You're not serious." Her father remained stiff as a scarecrow in her peripheral vision.

"Very," she said, glancing at Law, who looked as relieved as a man who had marched all the way to the gallows only to receive his pardon.

Parker Kane waved a hand as if he could dispel her declaration like so much smoke. "There's no need to be so impulsive. Decisions like these require time. Careful consideration. We'd discussed your path to CFO only this spring. Have you reflected on how this will affect your career?"

"Many times over." And this was true. She was convinced that no one thought faster and more clearly than a woman with a positive pregnancy test in her hand.

"Then there's your personal life to consider," he continued. "Your future prospects. Finding someone willing and able to raise someone else's child could prove just as difficult as raising a child alone."

Half-moons of fingernail dug into Marlowe's palms as the surge of white-hot rage shot through her. His complete dismissal of Law as either a potential parent or partner. The sickening irony. The self-delusion. The utter conceit.

"How dare *you* stand there and lecture *me* on what it takes to be a good parent?" Her voice quaked with emotion, ceasing her father's pigeon-like pacing.

He blinked at her, a maddening I-beg-your-pardon effrontery stretching his thin lips.

"*You*, who ignored and criticized and demeaned Samuel until he thought his best shot at getting your attention was pushing his own brother out of the family company. *You*, who lavished Mason with attention and praise while shoehorning him into a role that fit your image but made him so miserable he was ready to burn his own world down to get out of it. *You*, who despite how many trophies I won or honors I earned, never even saw me at all until I was engaged to the *Neil Farnsworth Campbell*," she spit, injecting each syllable of that name with venom. "Which is why I stayed engaged to him for so much longer than I should have. Not because I was afraid of losing him. Because I was afraid of losing *you*."

Hot tears rolled down her cheeks, and she dashed them away artlessly, like a furious child.

"I may not know how this is going to affect my career or my life, but I know one thing for damn sure. With Law as a father, my child will *never* know that kind of pain."

Parker Kane looked like he'd been sucker punched. Law, only slightly less winded and even more shocked.

"This may have been an accident," she continued, "but it isn't a mistake."

On a beleaguered sigh, her father folded his hands behind his back and paced toward the window. Just as he had every time she or her brothers had failed him in some irreparable way.

"Please," she said with a vehemence that startled both of them. "Please don't walk away from me. Not now."

He froze, as elegant and still as one of the many sculptures dotting Fair Weather Hall's neatly manicured gardens.

She spoke, past caring whether her words mattered at all, needing to say them *for* herself if not *to* him.

"All day, I couldn't stop thinking about what it would be like if Mom could have been here. What she would have worn. How beautiful she would have looked dancing with Samuel." Her throat tightened and she paused. Breathed.

"I thought about the things I could have asked her. What she could have told me about what it was like being pregnant for the first time. She never talked about that." Marlowe took a cautious step toward him, her arms hugged around her middle. "Do you remember?"

Her father blinked twice. An aperture opening on the past.

"I was working as the line supervisor at the Kane Confections warehouse in Hoboken when she found out. She brought me lunch in an old-fashioned picnic basket." His eyes misted, reflecting the glowing gold of the lamp by the window. "We sat at an old stone table overlooking the Hudson. She took out a thermos of coffee. Instead of sharing it from the cup, she took a mug out of the basket. It said—" His voice broke off as his prominent Adam's apple bobbed. "It said...Number One Dad."

Irony enough for a thousand lifetimes.

"When did you find out she was having twins?" she asked, wanting so badly to stay in this memory. To extract every detail.

"About five months along. She had been rereading *The Maltese Falcon* at the time. When we learned they were boys, she said that whichever twin was born first, she wanted to name Samuel. The second, Mason. She thought Perry sounded too stuffy."

Marlowe had to marvel inwardly at the intuition that had guided her choice.

"Chocolate-covered cherries," her father half whispered. "Those awful, syrupy chocolate-covered cherries Kane Foods always put out during the holidays. That's the only craving she had. I used to bring home boxes of them."

To think of her parents so young and in love was as strange as imagining her father as a line supervisor in the confections division, despite the fact that the Kane fortune had already been well established by two generations at that point.

"This isn't the way I expected it would happen or how I thought I would tell you, but…" Marlowe looked to Law. All traces of the bristling vigilance he'd displayed since her father's unexpected arrival had melted away, replaced by something softer. Sadder. Nostalgic, almost. "I want to do this. I don't know how it's all going to work out, exactly, but I know it will."

With this, memory's spell was broken.

"You've been exceptional at everything you've ever attempted, Marlowe. I'm certain being a mother will be no different."

The man who had been both tyrant and titan in her personal mythology stood stunned and rigid when she surged forward to hug him.

"Thank you, Father," she said, pressing her wet cheek against the starched fabric of his shirt.

He patted her back before releasing the embrace, recovering his composure as quickly as a cat. "Well, I think they'll be getting on with the toasts soon."

Marlowe tucked the sage-green tie she'd disheveled into his tuxedo vest. "We'll be right down," she said.

Acknowledgment of the word *we* flickered across his face before he nodded and turned, walking toward the door.

Then, to her endless wonder, Parker Kane stopped before Law to offer his hand.

She read the conflicting thoughts behind Law's amber eyes as they flicked downward. He had absolutely no reason to take it. Not after the way her father had treated him. Actively plotted against him. Outright insulted him.

He took it anyway.

Because that was the kind of man he was. That was the kind of father he would be. And he needed to know it.

The heavy door sighed closed with a click like a movie clapboard.

Action.

Law hummed with spent adrenaline, physically exhausted and mentally wiped despite having done nothing but stand in one place for fifteen minutes. But the restraint it had required would see him through a marathon.

Standing by as Parker Kane talked down to his daughter. Keeping his jaw wired shut as he questioned Law's right to breathe the same air as he did.

That had required restraint.

Though not nearly as much as keeping himself welded to the spot when Marlowe had announced she intended to have his baby. He had wanted to hold her so badly his arms had actually ached. Be a physical shield between her and the world. To gather her and the life within her as close to his body as possible.

Still did, but needed this, too, to be her choice.

"Are you okay?" Law pushed away from the wall but preserved the distance between them.

"You were right," she said, not answering his question. Arms still hugged protectively around her middle, she lifted her red-rimmed eyes to his. "When you called me a coward."

He winced, though she spoke the word to him more softly than he'd spoken it to her. "I didn't mean that."

"Yes," she insisted. "You did. And you were right. I was terrified." Huffing out a breath, she offered him a nervous smile. "I *am* terrified. Truth be told."

He nodded slowly. Was he terrified? No. But visiting the neighboring village. "Having a baby is—"

"I'm terrified of *you*, Law. Terrified of what you make me see about myself."

"Marlowe, you don't—"

She held up a hand just as he had. "You had your say. Now let me have mine."

His chest expanded on a bracing inhalation. A muscle ticked in his jaw as he attempted to keep his face neutral. "Go ahead."

"You asked about what happened between us while I was at 4 Thieves, and you should know that I went there intending to do exactly what my father sent me to do. With the information I gathered, I could have done it. Remy was right about that part."

Law narrowed his eyes at the mention of his brother's name. "I'd still like to break him in half for what he said to you that morning."

"He was trying to protect you, Law. To protect the distillery and its employees. What I did—it was selfish and irresponsible."

"I seem to remember there being two of us involved in the doing." His voice glowed with a husky heat.

"But not two of us sharing the consequences. That's why I left. Because what I felt with you, *for* you, was real. And I couldn't be just another person in your life that took something from you they couldn't give back."

"You didn't," he insisted.

"I would have. Without meaning to, I would have. I didn't know how to do anything else. That's what I meant when I said you helped me see things about myself. Understanding that helped me see things about you, too." Her lovely long arms relaxed, and he couldn't stop his eyes from sinking to her middle, still flat beneath the fabric of her dress. She closed the distance between them, her hands molding to his jaw, forcing him to find her eyes before he could find breath. "The thing is, I'm not sure you understand how absolutely amazing you really are."

Law hadn't blushed since the eighth grade and probably wouldn't have recognized the sensation if he didn't feel like someone had set a match to the tips of his ears.

"To think of what you endured as a child, what you overcame as a teenager, what you've built as a man. To have lived through all the pain your father put you through and yet *still* find room in your heart to forgive the brother who'd betrayed you after he'd put the business you pulled yourself up from the bootstraps to build in jeopardy? Do you have the first clue how rare that is? How rare *you* are?"

Sweat broke out between his shoulder blades, sticking his dress shirt to his back. He loosened his tie and tugged his collar away from his neck, positive he could feel steam venting from it. "You really don't have to do this."

He dearly wished she wouldn't.

Insults bounced off him like bullets off ballistic rubber.

Praise, he'd had no occasion to build up a tolerance for.

"My point is, any child would be lucky to have you. *I* would be lucky to have you, Law." Her eyes skated downward, filming with tears. "If you're still willing to have me."

Law notched a knuckle under her chin, running his thumb over the shoreline of her jaw as his lips hovered just above hers. "You're already mine."

He slid his fingers into the silk of her hair, cradling her head as he claimed her mouth in a greedy rush. She met his hunger for hunger, thirst for thirst, in a raw reunion that left them both panting.

"We need to put in an appearance downstairs," she breathed.

Grappling to keep his heated blood from pooling behind the zipper of his too-tailored slacks, Law smoothed the hair he'd rumpled. "How long does this appearance need to be?"

"Long enough to hear the toasts and grab a slice of cake." Her beautiful, slim fingers gripped the top of his tie, snugging the knot against his neck. She looked at him below eyelids lowered with lust, her irises glowing like pilot lights. "That we can eat in bed."

"I plan on eating dinner first." Leaning close to her ear, he brushed his kiss-warmed lips over the delicate lobe. "PS—you're dinner."

She arched an eyebrow at him as she took his offered elbow. "All six courses?"

Law opened the door and steered them toward the elevator. "Seven has always been my lucky number."

Epilogue

Marlowe sucked in a breath as the gel squelched onto her skin, as cold on her belly as Law's hand was warm around her fingers.

"You couldn't have warmed that first?" Law, hunkered on a stool beside the examination table, had watched the preparations for her ultrasound with keen interest, having apparently appointed himself quality and assurance manager of her comfort.

A development the technician appeared to be less than thrilled about.

"Relax." Marlowe reached across her paper gown–covered chest to pat his tensed jaw.

"I am relaxed," he insisted, almost kicking over a tray of instruments in his determination to casually cross an ankle over his knee, then almost upending it again in his attempt to right them.

She and the tech shared a knowing glance.

Alas, spaces dedicated to female matters were rarely built to comfortably house a man of Law's gladiatorial proportions.

The tech lifted the ultrasound wand from the automaton next to the bed and turned to them with an expectant look. "Ready?" she asked.

"Yes," Law answered before she'd finished pronouncing the *y*. He leaned forward on his stool, adorably eager, staring at the still-black screen.

At barely two months in, it was still too early to determine the sex, so Marlowe suspected his excitement had its roots elsewhere. *Elsewhere*, like believing this was really happening. That the pregnancy test she'd found him staring at in the predawn light the morning after Samuel's wedding had told him the truth.

If it hadn't been then, it surely could be now.

In the four days Law had been in Philadelphia, they'd rarely left the bed. Partly because of the fatigue that arrived after the wedding and partly because of the overactive sex drive that arrived with it. Law had no objections to obliging, despite the now-predictable bouts of morning sickness. Which, amazingly, did nothing whatsoever to dampen his ardor despite insisting on holding her hair back while she retched into the bowl.

The screen crackled, then filled with a swarming gray-white static as the technician moved the wand slowly over her slightly rounded belly. All at once, a dark pool appeared at its center, and the wand halted abruptly on the tech's barely audible squeak.

"What?" The paper beneath Law's elbow tore as he leaned around to get a better look. "What is it?"

"There," the technician said, pointing to the screen with the blue-gloved tip of one finger. "You see?"

Marlowe saw.

In that inky-black pond floated not one but *two* gray, bean-shaped tadpoles.

Twins.

Law released her hand, rising to his feet as slowly as a man in a trance. For a moment, his broad back obscured her view of the screen, and then he turned to her, his face thunderstruck.

"Twins," the tech announced when neither of them had spoken. "*Identical* twins."

A laugh and sob tangled behind the fingers fastened to Marlowe's mouth in shock. Law returned to her side, captured her other hand and kissed it, held it against his cheek.

Keeping the wand where it was, the technician reached for a second, this one shaped more like a flat-headed microphone, pressing it below and farther toward the center of her belly.

She heard them. Two distinct beats, chugging in a syncopated rhythm. Call and response.

Knowing when the heart begins.

Now she had three.

No wonder, then, that she felt herself full to the eye-brims with emotion, the tears spilling over when she turned her head slightly to look at the ultrasound screen.

She stared, transfixed. First at the monitor, then at the man by her side. Wonder shaved years away from his face and she saw what he must have looked like as a boy. Tufts of dark hair feathered by the breeze off the bayou. A wide unselfconscious smile lifting the corners of his lips. The unbearable vulnerability of joy in a life that had known so little. It filled her with a protective surge unlike any she had ever known.

"Will you marry me, Law?"

His eyes were slow to shift from the monitor to her face. "What did you say?"

"Will you marry me?" she repeated.

An endearingly canine expression of confusion lit his features. "Are you serious?"

"Have you ever known me not to be?"

The technician re-holstered the wands, wiped the gel from Marlowe's belly and politely excused herself.

"That's not how this is supposed to work," Law said. "There's no ring. And I haven't even—"

"Asked my father for my hand?" she supplied.

"I wouldn't go that far." His voice simmered with still-present, but greatly reduced, animosity.

In the weeks since learning of Marlowe's pregnancy, Parker Kane had proved an unlikely ally. Offering the use of a Kane Foods corporate jet for the days Law needed to be on-site at the distillery.

Law had refused, naturally, but it had been a nice gesture.

Especially the part where her father had hinted that, should someone want to divide time between Fincastle and Philadelphia, the Sugar High would make short work of the journey.

Marlowe didn't know just yet what she wanted where her career was concerned, but about Laurent Renaud, she had no doubts.

"Would you move to Fincastle? Or just go back and forth? Or—"

"I've always thought the country would be a nice place to raise a family," she said.

From her blissed-out cloud of oxytocin, Marlowe watched this word work on him.

"You would do that?" he asked, as if she were offering to step in front of a speeding train rather than relocate her home base five hours away.

"For you, yes." She squeezed his large, heavy hand and set it on her belly. "And for them. So they can live where there are trees for rope swings over a pond…"

"Maybe a corral for a horse or two," Law said, picking up the thread.

"And a cousin to play with," she replied, adding a new loop to the chain of the dream Law and Remy had pieced together as boys when the future had been the only tolerable place to live.

Law leaned in, fixing her with the same heated gaze that had set her aflame the first time she saw him across the hall of her childhood home. "Marlowe Kane, marrying you sounds a lot better than fine."

* * * * *

*Look for all the Kane Heirs novels
from Cynthia St. Aubin and Harlequin Desire!*

Corner Office Confessions
Secret Lives After Hours
Bad Boy with Benefits

COMING NEXT MONTH FROM

HARLEQUIN

DESIRE

#2911 ONE CHRISTMAS NIGHT
Texas Cattleman's Club: Ranchers and Rivals
by Jules Bennett

Ryan Carter and Morgan Grandin usually fight like cats and dogs—until one fateful night at a Texas Cattleman's Club masquerade ball. Now will an unexpected pregnancy make these hot-and-heavy enemies permanent lovers?

#2912 MOST ELIGIBLE COWBOY
Devil's Bluffs • by Stacey Kennedy

Brokenhearted journalist Adeline Harlow is supposed to write an exposé on Colter Ward, Texas's Sexiest Bachelor, *not* fall into bed with him enthusiastically and repeatedly! If only it's enough to break their no-love-allowed rule for a second chance at happiness...

#2913 A VALENTINE FOR CHRISTMAS
Valentine Vineyards • by Reese Ryan

Prodigal son Julian Brandon begrudgingly returns home to fulfill a promise. Making peace with his troubled past and falling for sophisticated older woman Chandra Valentine aren't part of the plan. But what is it they say about best-laid plans...?

#2914 WORK-LOVE BALANCE
Blackwells of New York • by Nicki Night

When gorgeous TV producer Jordan Chambers offers Ivy Blackwell the chance of a lifetime, the celebrated heiress and social media influencer wonders if she can handle his tempting offer...and the passion that sizzles between them!

#2915 TWO RIVALS, ONE BED
The Eddington Heirs • by Zuri Day

Stakes can't get much higher for attorneys Maeve Eddington and Victor Cortez in the courtroom...or in the bedroom. With family fortunes on the line, these rivals will go to any lengths to win. But what if love is the ultimate prize?

#2916 BILLIONAIRE MAKEOVER
The Image Project • by Katherine Garbera

When PR whiz Olive Hayes transforms scruff CEO Dante Russo into the industry's sexiest bachelor, she realizes she's equally vulnerable to his charms. But is she falling for her new creation or the man underneath the makeover?

YOU CAN FIND MORE INFORMATION ON UPCOMING HARLEQUIN TITLES, FREE EXCERPTS AND MORE AT HARLEQUIN.COM.

HDCNM1022

SPECIAL EXCERPT FROM

(H) HARLEQUIN

DESIRE

Thanks to violinist Megan Han's one-night fling with her father's new CFO, Daniel Pak, she's pregnant! No one can know the truth—especially not her matchmaking dad, who'd demand marriage. If only her commitment-phobic not-so-ex lover would open his heart...

Read on for a sneak peek at
One Night Only
by Jayci Lee.

The sway of Megan's hips mesmerized him as she glided down the walkway ahead of him. He caught up with her in three long strides and placed his hand on her lower back. His nostrils flared as he caught a whiff of her sweet floral scent, and reason slipped out of his mind.

He had been determined to keep his distance since the night she came over to his place. He didn't want to betray Mr. Han's trust further. And it wouldn't be easy for Megan to keep another secret from her father. The last thing he wanted was to add to her already full plate. But when he saw her standing in the garden tonight—a vision in her flowing red dress—he knew he would crawl through burning coal to have her again.

She reached for his hand, and he threaded his fingers through hers, and she pulled them into a shadowy alcove and pressed her back against the wall. He placed his hands on either side of her head and stared at her face until his eyes adjusted to the dark. He sucked in a sharp breath when she slid her palms over his chest and wrapped her arms around his neck.

"I don't want to burden you with another secret to keep from your father." He held himself in check even as desire pumped through his veins.

"I think fighting this attraction between us is the bigger burden," she whispered. His head dipped toward her of its own volition, and she wet her lips. "What are you doing, Daniel?"

"Surviving," he said, his voice a low growl. "Because I can't live through another night without having you."

She smiled then—a sensual, triumphant smile—and he was lost.

Don't miss what happens next in…
One Night Only
by Jayci Lee.

Available December 2022 wherever
Harlequin Desire books and ebooks are sold.

Harlequin.com

HDEXP1022

Get 4 FREE REWARDS!

We'll send you 2 FREE Books plus 2 FREE Mystery Gifts.

FREE
Value Over
$20

Both the **Harlequin® Desire** and **Harlequin Presents®** series feature compelling novels filled with passion, sensuality and intriguing scandals.

YES! Please send me 2 FREE novels from the Harlequin Desire or Harlequin Presents series and my 2 FREE gifts (gifts are worth about $10 retail). After receiving them, if I don't wish to receive any more books, I can return the shipping statement marked "cancel." If I don't cancel, I will receive 6 brand-new Harlequin Presents Larger-Print books every month and be billed just $6.05 each in the U.S. or $6.24 each in Canada, a savings of at least 10% off the cover price or 6 Harlequin Desire books every month and be billed just $4.80 each in the U.S. or $5.49 each in Canada, a savings of at least 13% off the cover price. It's quite a bargain! Shipping and handling is just 50¢ per book in the U.S. and $1.25 per book in Canada.* I understand that accepting the 2 free books and gifts places me under no obligation to buy anything. I can always return a shipment and cancel at any time by calling the number below. The free books and gifts are mine to keep no matter what I decide.

Choose one: ☐ **Harlequin Desire**
(225/326 HDN GRTW)

☐ **Harlequin Presents Larger-Print**
(176/376 HDN GQ9Z)

Name (please print)

Address   Apt. #

City   State/Province   Zip/Postal Code

Email: Please check this box ☐ if you would like to receive newsletters and promotional emails from Harlequin Enterprises ULC and its affiliates. You can unsubscribe anytime.

> Mail to the **Harlequin Reader Service:**
> **IN U.S.A.:** P.O. Box 1341, Buffalo, NY 14240-8531
> **IN CANADA:** P.O. Box 603, Fort Erie, Ontario L2A 5X3

Want to try 2 free books from another series? Call 1-800-873-8635 or visit www.ReaderService.com.

Love Harlequin romance?

DISCOVER.

Be the first to find out about promotions, news and exclusive content!

f Facebook.com/HarlequinBooks

y Twitter.com/HarlequinBooks

O Instagram.com/HarlequinBooks

P Pinterest.com/HarlequinBooks

You Tube YouTube.com/HarlequinBooks

ReaderService.com

EXPLORE.

Sign up for the Harlequin e-newsletter and download a free book from any series at
TryHarlequin.com

CONNECT.

Join our Harlequin community to share your thoughts and connect with other romance readers!
Facebook.com/groups/HarlequinConnection

HARLEQUIN

Heartfelt or thrilling, passionate or uplifting—Harlequin is more than just happily-ever-after.

With twelve different series to choose from and new books available every month, you are sure to find stories that will move you, uplift you, inspire and delight you.

IF YOU ENJOYED THIS BOOK
WE THINK YOU WILL ALSO LOVE

HARLEQUIN

PRESENTS

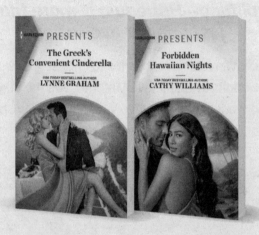

Escape to exotic locations where passion knows no bounds.

Welcome to the glamorous lives of royals and billionaires, where passion knows no bounds. Be swept into a world of luxury, wealth and exotic locations.

8 NEW BOOKS AVAILABLE EVERY MONTH!